LEGACY

By the same author:

No Fancy Life, The Book Guild, 2001
Tric-Trac, The Book Guild, 2003
Doon The Road, The Book Guild, 2006

LEGACY

Charlotte Grey

Book Guild Publishing

Sussex, England

First published in Great Britain in 2009 by
The Book Guild
Pavilion View
19 New Road
Brighton, BN1 1UF

Typesetting in Palatino by
Keyboard Services, Luton, Bedfordshire

Printed in Great Britain by
CPI Antony Rowe

A catalogue record for this book is available from
The British Library

ISBN 978 1 84624 296 0

It does not matter that my house is rather small;
One cannot sleep in more than one room:

It does not matter that I have not many horses;
One cannot ride on two horses at once:

As fortunate as me among the people of the world
possibly one would find seven out of ten,

As contented as me among a hundred men
Look as you may, you will not find one.

AD 835 – Chinese poem translated by Arthur Waley.

Glossary

aa	all
aht	out
allus	always
brae	hill, slope
bust	burst
cawf	calf
cowd	cold
dae	do
Dam Stones	weir across river Wharfe
dee	die
deid	dead
dunt	does not
eneuch	enough
fin	when
fit	what
fudder	move excitedly
girt	great
grun	ground
guid	good
gyaun	going
hale jing-bang	whole lot

haudin' oot	maintaining
hefted	strongly attached to a particular place
Howe	Howe of Alford, Aberdeenshire
kitchie-deem	kitchen-maid
knaw	know
langsyne	long ago
leal-herted	loyal
mair	more
maun	must
mither	mother
nae	no, not
nawther	neither
noan	not, none
nobbut	only
ony	only
richt	right
roarin'	crying
siller	money
skelp	hit, wallop
sleekit	smooth
speer	ask
spik	talk, gossip
steer	stir, bustle
stot	castrated bullock
stracht	street
stramash	uproar, commotion
summat	something

tak tent	give heed to
teem	empty
tellin'	reprimand
thowt	thought
trauchled	overburdened
wid	would
wint	want
wirk	work
yestreen	yesterday evening

Introduction

It was different yet at every step it felt familiar. Passing the end house of Grangefield Avenue she half expected to see the old lady who had taught her aunt at the National School. Further on was a house where a shop used to be. On the opposite side of the road the high wall round the big house had gone and small houses were built on the sweeping lawns hidden then. She remembered allotments on a road; now, it was houses and a mere step to reach Main Street. The cricket field was there, but on the right of Grange Road a doctors' surgery and car park and a library were new to her and the park itself different, all opened up to a view of Main Street and traffic. Fences had made the park quite separate, trees grown close hid clusters of rhododendrons, lovely to see in springtime. Inside them and in other old trees children found places where low branches made a seat or pine needles a soft floor in the houses they imagined. Now a well-kept bowling green offered other pleasure, flowerbeds were bright, but a box from someone's supper and oddments of litter fouled the grass.

Past the Round House and the former council offices she went to post a letter telling her husband she would stay to show people the house; one or two people were interested, and with luck she would be home quite soon.

Chapter 1

The old-fashioned key turned in an oiled lock. There was another key for a Yale lock above it, and a chain dangled inside – Aunt Mary had not intended to be burgled or to fall victim to the wrong sort of caller. A lobby of minute size with a door leading to the living room: she had a vague memory of this or a similar door with glass panels covered in coloured paper, but a bright diamond pattern had been dimmed by a coat of varnish.

She made tea and took from a barrel-shaped tin marked Huntley & Palmers a biscuit fresh enough to be one of her aunt's last purchases. It was sad thinking of that. Everything had happened so quickly, the heart giving out and the hospital unable to do anything; her exit with minimal fuss in keeping with the way she had lived.

Keys handed over had a third key on the ring, its use explained when the next-door neighbour produced a small box like a miniature trunk made of olive wood. Aunt Mary had left the keys and box with Sandra, and must have had absolute faith in the young woman who whisked through the old lady's chores 'like a breath of fresh air', her aunt had written when age began to catch up on her.

Sandra's appearance had been something of a surprise, a brief skirt, yellow hair, and big hooped earrings reflecting every move of a pert little head. She had what folk in Aberdeenshire would describe as a fine seam of teeth and honesty shone from a smiling face. Aunt Mary knew a good Yorkshire lass when she saw one, and it was unlikely the third key had been turned in the olivewood box. At

3

the moment she did not want to examine the contents: a cursory glance showed a mass of paper, bank statements, receipted accounts, an inventory with pathetically few items. Old letters there could make painful reading when she herself had done little to enhance a rather solitary life, always too busy, unable or unwilling to make the effort to visit.

The agent was bringing people to view but there was nothing to do in preparation after Sandra's thorough 'going-over' and if necessary she would come in and give the place a 'tickle-up' later. More than a good neighbour, Sandra had been a veritable treasure for her aunt, who had made some provision in the will: perhaps she should have more, given in a way which did not offend.

The agent or the people themselves were not punctual but it did not matter, she was content to wait on the broad old-fashioned sofa purchased at Arthur Darbyson's in Main Street, where everybody in the village went for such things. Her aunt had been very proud of it and the two armchairs, all kept pristine by fitted covers rather than easier throws. A small enamelled Yorkist range replaced a large cast-iron one which needed blacklead polish. Most people had changed to neat gas fires, but the open fire and adjoining oven satisfied Aunt Mary and her living room had oozed comfort. 'I'm snug as a bug in a rug,' she would say if you suggested central heating. The agent approved of the range, said people would consider it a 'feature', which would have brought a wry chuckle and the quote, 'There's nowt so queer as fowk!'

Such thoughts were interrupted by a firm assault on the door knocker. They had arrived, people holding brochures and the young man in charge. It was difficult to say he ushered them in, because the tiny lobby and the room itself had no space for gesture; however, he was a dominant force, helped by a strong aftershave scent.

The viewers were young, both tall and thin and they seemed uncertain, causing a doubt that they would want the house. A smart flat with white sofas and designer-style glass table might suit them better. The agent was quick to scoop them up the stairs to see the bedrooms, two with the third now a bathroom; Aunt Mary had agreed to this. They visited the kitchen – neat it was, but hardly up to modern standards. In the old days it had been the 'back kitchen' and had a stone sink with a copper boiler alongside and the floor had been stone as well. She could remember bright clip rugs lessening the cold in winter. A long pantry had taken all foodstuffs and pots and pans and where the ascending stair made an alcove, a stone slab kept things cool, in addition to a metal 'safe' with the door pierced with tiny holes, the nearest thing to a refrigerator. Aunt Mary had improved on the pantry but not much else.

A peep at the back garden, just grass, a path, and that was it. They left, the young man offering his hand and the girl already gliding out, turning with a rather sweet smile and an inaudible goodbye or thank-you. In a final whiff of aftershave the agent volunteered that they thought the range 'super'.

She had noticed some sort of communication as between familiars, with lips scarcely moving and heads inclined together, but had not heard the words. She looked the agent firmly in the eye. 'Of course,' she said, 'it is something of a "feature".' For a moment he hesitated, blinked, and then with another handshake followed his quarry.

She relaxed on the Arthur Darbyson sofa and thought about the possibility of a sale. It seemed unlikely. A source of irritation to her aunt, and her parents too, that young people who had most things 'handed to them on a plate' did not speak well, their voices inaudible except to one another, not clearly articulated or produced, the lips lazy and the face void of expression. A rueful thought came: influenced by this house, I agree with them, think the same.

She stared at the range and became inspired – a clip rug! It needs a clip rug in front to show it off! She had seen such rugs advertised, Sandra would know. Sandra did, looking a tad curious. A stall in Skipton market had them now and again from an arts and craft place, quite expensive.

'Nae problem. When's the market? Come with me Sandra? We'll have a day out!'

Chapter 2

The clip rug looked perfect, absolutely the thing for the 'feature' and for the house itself. They were lucky to find one more or less the right size – the girl running the stall said they sold quickly, and the lady making them was snowed under with orders for all sizes. She kept the rug for them while they had a good look round and it had been fascinating. Skipton market was a treasure trove with everything you could think of there for the asking. 'Owt yer fancy,' they might say here; at home it would be 'Aa ye wid need.' Locally sourced meat, bacon, cheeses, vegetables, plants, flowers, and from elsewhere clothes, hats, scarves, trinkets, sweeties on offer to the crowds of people milling round. It all seemed good tempered, the stallholders cheerful and polite, with really comical repartee. She had enjoyed the market and Rackhams, a department store where they had lunch, though Sandra said there were cheaper places where you could get very good fish and chips. Sandra looked at a dress on their way out and, peering at the ticket, said, 'My God, you'd have to be barmy!'

Driving away past Skipton Castle reminded her of going there by appointment to see antiquarian books before they were married when John had this interest. She told Sandra how they had driven up and been admitted by a uniformed gatekeeper who touched his cap and directed them. John did buy the books he wanted, but the memorable thing about the visit was being shown a book so rare that it was one of only a few in existence. The owner handled it wearing gloves and turned the pages for them, showing pictures of birds in the most exquisite colours, page after page of them all painted by the artist Audubon. She had never forgotten the book, valued then at many thousands of pounds; today it must be reckoned beyond price. She wondered if it remained in the castle.

'John still has his books, Sandra, but as a hard-up farmer, has given up buying. One of these days he'll probably sell them to buy cows.' She made Sandra laugh by telling how they left; the stout gate opened for them, the keeper touching his hat in a farewell salute, and John saying, 'How do you feel about that, Duchess?'

Afterwards, as they drove towards Ilkley she felt a longing for home, reinforced by the green of hills and fields and animals grazing or peacefully cudding, and became silent. Sandra was perceptive. 'You'll sell in a flash, luv, with that rug down.'

And now she was waiting again for the agent and viewers he said were very interested. The house was spic and span and the rug was placed ready to be admired.

She knew as soon as the men entered the house that she did not want them to buy it; wished she could stand in front of the 'feature' to stop them noticing it and snatch the rug out of sight. No. No. No. They were not right and she wanted them away. Not that they showed any wish to linger – they gave only a cursory look round and paid little attention to the agent. Why had they come? Expensive clothes, hard eyes, very unlikely to choose a little terraced house like this to live in or even as a holiday cottage. What could be their plan, the motive for the visit? Buy to Let? Investment? It was too small for any grandiose schemes. Was it something more sinister one might read about in the papers, immigrants, refugees, all crowded in? Perhaps the agent read her mind, as he did not persevere with them and muttered that he would be back shortly with other clients. Drinking the percolated coffee she had intended to offer, it was funnier in recollection. Such smart city gents wanting a tiny terraced house? 'Sleekit scoonrels' folks at home would consider 'nae guid te deal with'. And she agreed. She felt better after making a judgement entirely without basis. On the plus side, now she knew not to rely too much on the agent's description of people brought to view. She decided to take a walk to get the 'crooks' out of mind.

She turned right and went down Back Lane, familiar in memory but now with more houses, the smithy gone and no Mr Pullen in his little green hut selling fruit and ice cream. Into view came a pleasant space with trees and flowers and the old church not far away. She decided to sit and take in the changes, choosing a seat which had a label saying something about a dear wife. An old man passed, hesitated and came back to sit with her, his dog slow to arrange itself at his feet. She wondered if she had usurped their usual place.

''Ello there' came in the way of friendliness and perhaps a little curiosity. Then 'Grand day!' and she agreed. 'Just passin' thru, are ye?' She explained her presence, and to her surprise and pleasure, he had known her aunt. 'She wor a grand lass, Mary, that she wor!' A fair summing up of Aunt Mary.

'This little park is new, I don't remember it at all.'

His face broke into a confidential smile. 'Reet in wun sense an' wrong in t'other! It's new, or nobbut a few years owd, but nut a park!' She waited. 'It's the Village Green!' Emphasis made a title of it. Mischief to the smile and a little slyness – 'We managed afore, nivver gev it a minnit's thowt, but nah we're up wi'all t'others an' 'ave wun. We 'ave a Village Green!'

It was familiar, the way he talked, going back to a time when her grandparents and uncles and friends spoke like that. Not only the accent, but the way of thinking, looking at things in a quirky way, amused as if to prove that you are not fooled, know what's afoot and nobody pulls the wool over your eyes. To some extent she sympathised with that.

'We're on t'Tourist Route, as well!' Again capital letters implied. 'Gateway to the Dales so they say, but it's a fair owd trek if ye've no car!'

There was a sudden squealing of brakes and smart cars pulled up outside the hotel which used to be called the Malt Shovel. Young people spilled out of the cars, laughing, fooling with one another, loud confident voices ... 'Nigel, you idiot, stop it! ... Emma, wait! ... Who's paying darling? ... Come on, you lot, I'm thirsty! ...'

A scowl over the genial face, a different tone: 'We git a lot like them, an' all. Money te burn, think theer it!'

Again this way of looking at the young, thinking they have it too easy, have too much money, perhaps envying their energy, their beauty...

Her companion had decided to go home. 'Cum on then Tiger!' He smiled, waiting for the irony to sink in as his dog gathered its old arthritic legs for the walk. A little more to say, 'My missus'll nut thank me fer being ower long, she likes te keep me under observation!'

She was glad his missus was there and was not the one the seat was 'in memory of'. He looked cared for. A stick pointed towards the smart cars – 'We get such as yon winin' an' dinin'. A place up Main Street's in t'Good

10

Food Guide or summat!' Tiger under way. A touch at the cap and just one thing more, nonchalantly over the shoulder: 'We got pop'lar after t' Powers-That-Be shifted the river...'

Chapter 3

She awoke early with light shining on her face because she had forgotten to draw the curtains – they never did that on the farm with no houses near. She thought the bed was the same one she'd slept in once or twice when her parents had to make room for relatives visiting. It seemed momentous at the time, having a suitcase with her nightdress and a change of knickers and socks; in reality, it meant moving from the other end of the village and having breakfast with Aunt Mary. Later, after her family moved away, she had come for a fortnight of school holidays with more baggage, including homework her aunt promised to supervise. It was years ago and yet so familiar as if she had only to call out and Aunt Mary would tell her to hurry up and get dressed, her breakfast was waiting and she wanted things cleared away before leaving for work.

John had telephoned late last night saying all was well, he hadn't emptied the freezer yet and she could take her time, make a holiday of it. She told him about the city gents and about the nice old man and Tiger and he said she seemed to be living dangerously and asked about the scented agent. He had cheered her up, as intended, and it would be an idea to do what he suggested, get around a bit and not sit waiting for viewers. She decided to walk to the river rather than take the car. Summer and winter she had loved going to the Dam Stones – nothing there could have changed very much. She crossed Main Street at Iron Row and went along past cottages all very similar, with white-painted doors and black ironwork. She had no memory of such uniformity of doors and windows, or of hanging baskets, or roses round any door. Cars were parked in front of some cottages and garages for them were on the opposite side of the road. It was all very smart: her agent would describe the little houses as 'desirable', as on Aunt Mary's brochure, and a wry comment *that* would have brought.

Through the former gateway to Fisons' Mill were newish houses, but more of a surprise, a tunnel going beneath the bypass, the traffic noise very loud. It was fortunate she had decided to walk, as the tunnel was solely for the use of pedestrians or cyclists, though with evidence of a recent horse.

Aunt Mary had written to them about the bypass but they had not taken in the enormity of the change, the woodland and fields taken over, meadows and parkland lost. When she was very young the road back from the Dam Stones had seemed endless through pastureland as far as you could see, with fine old trees spreading shade. And quiet, only the sound of their feet, her own dragging, and sometimes the tap tap of the cane of a fishing net half-slipping from her fingers. Unique that time, had she been old enough to understand, before the world moved on to have cars for all and consequent noise and a great demand for land to build more and more houses for the people with cars.

Beyond the underpass there was the mill and its gatehouse where friends of her grandmother lived. She remembered an office with a switchboard and telephones and things to do with shutting the enormous gates. You

13

passed through this strange place to go into the house and the sitting room where she sat in silence while the grown-ups chatted, not giving Grandma any cause to grumble.

After the gatehouse and the mill the road was familiar, with vaguely remembered houses on the left, then all was different, the road coming to a stop until she found a gate and a path into a wood, its surface dry and soft and here and there roots of old trees poking through. The path led to what she realised was the former road shrunken in size, the hedges overgrown and on the right so high that she caught only a glimpse of the Goit. When the hedge was low and sparse the water had been close and dark and intimidating; there between gaps in paving at the road's edge to cause a shiver and the need to catch up with parents or whoever you were with. Today the water was still and gave a fetid smell, the Goit having no function for the people who made furniture and sold bathroom fittings, carpets and floor tiles in the mill buildings. The days of the wool merchants and the clattering machinery had gone, replaced by quieter enterprises.

As she walked there was a rustle of birds and a squirrel was aware of her; fields likely to yield a good crop of hay stretched into the distance, and a drift of water lilies shone from water thick with algae. The sound of a weir grew insistent and there she was at the Dam Stones.

As of old, water poured over the dam to what she knew as the 'Big Drop', and had been told was a bottomless pool. What implication of fearful depth, down, down, down, no end to the black water if you fell in. It was probably boys who projected this image, knowing her to be gullible. However, only good swimmers went in the Big Drop; there were safer places for children and a lower pool for the timid. But now a notice near the stepping stones said all bathing was prohibited, which was a pity,

14

for a good many youngsters had learned to swim at this spot before even thinking of challenging the Big Drop.

The stepping stones were different: uniform blocks replaced old random stones which had been easy to cross when the water was low but hazardous if the flow was strong, some totally covered, so you needed to stride out over them. The present ones were less picturesque but more efficient. And now there was talk of a bridge, pleasing to those who wanted one and campaigned for it, attracting support from those on the fringes of fame who jumped on any bandwagon. Farmers who owned the pleasant fields across the river should be aware – in Aberdeenshire, 'tak tent' was an expression used. Experience on the farm had been mixed. Some of the walkers with their rucksacks and bobble hats had not endeared themselves: John had to cope with litter and damage to fences and sometimes campers left opened tins with jagged edges highly dangerous to young stock. Not all the ramblers were like that, but with some you felt the Country Code was as alien to them as reading Proust.

She stood for a long time enjoying sight and sound of the great torrent of water pouring over the dam. Depending on the needs of the mill, only now and again had the full force of the river flowed over the barrier like that; at times, only one or two sections were opened to allow water through. Looking at sunlit fields on the other bank reminded her how it was in winter, with unbroken snow as far as you could see, the river dotted with ice and the stepping stones frosted. And all so quiet, not many people walking. Her father had insisted on taking the exercise. She remembered how hard it was to leave the warm fireside.

She decided to go back by Leatherbank as they used to do on the walks and was astonished when a woman with a surly expression accused her of parking a car in the wrong place. 'This is private!' she had barked. 'Can't you read?' So unexpected was this that she merely blinked and walked on past the offending car. The woman would see that looking sour and jumping out at harmless people was not the best way of dealing with a problem. There were more 'No Parking' and 'Private' signs on the way to Main Street and again a tunnel under the new road. The horse had chosen that way home too.

Main Street was uneventful, little grey houses and traffic, and near the centre of the village a sign for a nature reserve she might visit. Coming to Iron Row where she started off, on an impulse she went into a newly opened shop and bought sunflowers and other flowers which they promised to deliver.

Chapter 4

The next couple of days brought viewers, the first an unaccompanied lady arriving in a car more expensive than others parked along the terrace. Explaining that she owned several properties for renting, she asked to take a quick look. Easily done in Aunt Mary's house, the range and its new effects of rug and flowers noticed without comment and the Mercedes soon away, a whiff of good perfume the only reminder. After that came the agent and an older couple who took things more slowly and accepted coffee. It was hard to tell if this was a sign of interest or, having walked from the local office, they were glad to take the weight off their feet. The agent said the coffee was a treat because mostly he got instant and at home too, which made everybody smile. Relaxed, the man gave out that he was retiring soon and their plan was to downsize. Did this mean their own house had to be sold first? As they did not offer that information and the agent was carefully dabbing at his mouth with a nice white hanky, she did not ask. Perhaps one improved at selling houses the longer it took to find your buyer, but it was disagreeable to ask about money, as it implied can you afford my asking price, how solvent are you? John called any savings you tried to collect your 'kedge anchor' and both spoke of 'drop dead money', culled from reading about a child who hoarded pocket money with the idea of running away from home. Tactless to apply that term here and money hardly came into things at this stage. Afterwards, Sandra said it was always the quiet ones who had the cash; certainly these two were quiet enough. How Sandra knew was another question unasked.

How long the 'holiday' of selling the house was likely to last was difficult to foretell. The good neighbour did most of the chores but it was frustrating having to keep everything up to scratch and she was unused to sitting about. On the farm the amount of work exceeded the number of hands available and slave labour was her lot, her fate in this life, she claimed. Yet, here she was doing nothing… Rain patterned the windows, so walking was out. There was nothing for it but to get the box and sort out its contents. Into mind came a poem by Thomas Hardy in which the dead whisper to the living about their indifference to things: the squire's late wife, Lady Susan, offers – 'You may … ransack coffer, desk, bureau; quiz the few poor treasures hid there, con the letters kept by me.' She felt loth to look at her aunt's treasures.

The box was lovely; shaped like a little trunk, it had a sheen, perhaps the patina of age. Somehow foreign-looking, maybe a present from Dennis who, before a German submarine ended his young life, was engaged to be married to Aunt Mary. Mention of this tragedy was usually avoided. In her teens when she had sent a soulful letter about an unrequited love, her aunt had written by return of post saying, 'Don't be so daft, there's plenty more fish in the sea.' Wise words, but no other fish had surfaced for Aunt Mary.

Bank statements over a period of years and receipts kept for the required amount of time could be burned now in the empty grate; guarantees of household equipment were out of date so the grate could have these too. Bundles of letters, some faded cards, a visitors' book with a nice binding and at the bottom of the box a number of exercise books filled with neat writing. Sorting the box was going to take time and it was a task she did not relish. Reluctant to begin, she closed the lid and as her aunt must have done many times, ran her fingers over the smooth wood, admiring the crafted hinges making the perfect closure. The visitors' book with its title picked out in gold on the leather cover seemed the easiest option, and so it proved. Turning the pages brought familiar names, including her own, carefully written at first and later losing the rounded young look; she had not ventured any comment as others did. 'About time too! But better late than never' was Grandma's. After a while the names stopped and gave way to new purpose – Commonplace Book, her aunt had written in bold capital letters.

It was interesting to see verses from Wordsworth, Rupert Brooke, Byron, Yeats, Matthew Arnold and, more poignant, from Wilfred Owen and the war poets. Further blank pages before excerpts from the Bible, Blake, Shakespeare, and as if an afterthought, 'Life is a bridge, build no house on it' – where had that come from? There were pages with quotes from books and articles, H.G. Wells, Trollope, Henry James. Some of Aunt Mary's evenings may have been solitary but she had peopled them with good company. At the back of the book were definitions of words and phrases, terms like 'the Dog Days', the hottest days of summer, carefully explained in the neat handwriting as being named after the star Sirius, the brightest star in the constellation Canis Major. 'To the Egyptians the arrival of Sirius in the sky meant the start of the flooding season of the Nile; to the Romans the "caniculares dies" were days of intolerable heat, lethargy, sickness and disease, caused by the rising of the star...'

The book must be preserved and perhaps they could make time to add their own favourites like the little gems from the Doric she loved to collect. Aunt Mary had specifically mentioned the olivewood box in her will, left it in the hands of a trusted friend 'for my dear niece to dispose of the contents as she thinks fit'. You had to suspect a plan to keep the Commonplace Book going.

She sat for a long time and then put a match to the piled grate, watching the flames take hold to banish all trace of money coming in and going out, the ever careful husbanding of limited resources, nothing inviting risk, no extravagances. The house was a legacy generous enough without the kedge anchor money which should have gone on creature comforts, holidays, cruises perhaps, even a car like the Mercedes. The flames cast a glow over the tall flowers bought to enhance the room's appeal: foxgloves, lilies, long-stemmed carnations of a strange greenish colour, some pretty white flowers she did not know the name of and, brightest of all, the faces of three large sunflowers. Aunt Mary's house should have seen more flowers.

She thought of telephoning John but decided to wait – he would be pretty busy with her away. Sadness was inevitable here, and so was regret that she could have done more, taken time to visit, written more often; her aunt always loved news of the farm and replied to letters almost by return of post. For days she had been meaning to telephone and then it happened, out of the blue, the shock of it... 'Ye nivver ken the 'oor or the minit!' avowed the Scots and it was true of all deaths. But she must not burden John with her guilt. Words alleged to have been spoken by King Alfred the Great were appropriate: 'If thou hast a woe, tell it to thy saddlebag and ride on.' In effect she had to ride on, sound upbeat on the telephone, pretend to be enjoying the 'holiday'. Alongside that resolve,

she detected a small part of her brain registering King
Alfred for the Commonplace Book, and the Doric wisdom
could go in too.

Chapter 5

No appointments to view, no call from the agent.

She decided to go out rather than yearn for a whiff of aftershave. The delay was irritating, no one in need of a little house in what the brochures said was a much sought-after village, no rush for the gateway to the Dales the old man mentioned. Did the agent need a reminder? On the farm, John dealt with all awkward situations and, without a raised voice or any threat, people were left in no doubt as to what was required of them. In a really bad case there would be more steel and a certain straight-browed look that brooked no opposition. Thankfully she did not need anything like that, as yet. She had to smile at the thought of the agent under John's scrutiny. She put on shoes suitable for a damp walk and a raincoat as the sky had the threat of rain still to come. Today was her chance to see where they had 'shifted the river', look for the join between old and new. According to Sandra, the change to the river's course and the making of the bypass was a huge improvement; before it happened traffic on Main Street had been nose-to-tail and crossing the road a nightmare. Sensible in that case to make the new road, but you had to mourn the lost trees and the green walks by the river reduced to a minimum.

Reaching the church, on impulse she decided to go in. On the last visit she had worn school uniform, a hat and gloves, and made a great fuss about that, saying other girls did not, but unlike the river, Aunt Mary had remained unmoved.

The churchyard was levelled out, perhaps to make it easier to cut the grass and keep things tidy. It seemed smaller, and so did the carpeted entrance where a looped bellrope on the wall reminded her of cheerful men pulling hard to ring out the peal summoning you to prayer. If there had been a death, the deep note from one bell saddened you so you hurried past. The soft green carpet continued in the body of the church and footsteps made no echo, which seemed strange to her. Plain walls had lost the border of purple grapes children looked at while the words floated to heaven over their heads. More important was the absence of a great eagle whose shining wings unfolded to hold the Holy Book. When a reading was familiar it caught the attention, and 'Here endeth the lesson' rang out as people relaxed, shifting a little in the pews. It was strange now to see the pulpit in the eagle's place and the font brought from the rear to replace it, giving a complete change of focus for the sermon. She wondered if people remembered the eagle, or had it flown too long ago? The church looked clean and bright and was so much warmer: a long line of reverend gentlemen preaching here through many cold winters would have approved, but might regret the eagle. A memorial tablet for those lost in the 1914–1918 World War had family names, and another tablet recorded losses from the Second and other wars, Aunt Mary's Dennis among them. So many lives. *Pro patria mori*, they said, but this must sound hollow when the loss is yours.

She walked on past the corn mill, which looked deserted and did not seem to have the same function, the building much run-down. Through a little gate at the end of a muddy path she came to the new road, and crossing it was difficult when cars from Main Street and from the

Menston and Otley roads were moving at a rate of knots. She reached the river and walked along a path almost lost in a flourish of weeds, tall thistles, brambles aiming to cover everything, in effect, nature rampant. Pink flowers she did not recognise had a defiant beauty.

A couple of stone slabs to cross a ditch and there it was, what she had been told marked the join. The gateway was a rickety iron structure, pieces of wood meant to repair broken rails sagged, rotting and useless. Pushing at the gate, she walked into fields made narrow by the changes, the grass greyish and thistles unchecked. She knew exactly what John would have thought and no doubt said: 'Coos need better grass...' Their own herd gave strong protest when a field was not up to snuff. Cattle had left their mark but cannot have had much joy here. On the opposite bank beyond willows at the water's edge stretched pasture land which looked better, old trees offered shelter under a spread of low branches, the scene reminiscent of other times. A family of ducks dabbled where the willows dipped pale leaves and the water was quiet. People said they saw herons here, and more rarely the kingfisher. It was impossible to see where the new course joined the old river: no scars, nature had seen to it. Clouds were gathering and rain came, a hint at first and then what she knew as mizzling, the fine drizzle which could develop into real wet stuff. She made a purposeful way back through the weeds.

The house was colder than of late and it took seconds only to put a match to the carefully built fire. Today impressing viewers was not an issue, though come to think of it, a coal fire gave some appeal. She would make tea, eat and settle to write letters, or more usefully tackle the box again. The first of several closely written exercise books was in diary form. Perhaps Aunt Mary wanted a record for Dennis when he was on leave, of less important happenings or those untold because a problem might be well and truly solved before he got a letter mentioning it. So trivial things were listed, small mishaps, difficulties at her place of work, and with some relish the spats with her aunt who did not approve of either the engagement or of Mary living alone in the little house. Reading those bits did not surprise, Mary's aunt was her own grandmother whose tongue caused trouble, giving all members of the family scars to show. She read on until the writing stopped and did not resume. Pasted at the end of the book was the telegram giving news that Dennis was lost at sea... How sad, and how normal at the time, like the losses on the church memorials from all the wars before and after poor Dennis. But the other books. What about them? Aunt Mary had picked up her pen later and written about what?

It was getting late, the fire dying, and there was no point in building it up again. She wondered how often in those wartime evenings the fire had burned low in front of her aunt sitting not on the Arthur Darbyson sofa but on the old horsehair one she herself remembered because it had pricked so painfully at bare legs.

The telephone rang and it was John hitting the right moment even by accident. He sounded tired but pleased with himself for managing to get the VAT forms done, one of her own tasks normally. All was quiet on the farm, the beasts all checked; he described them in the steading as he said goodnight to them and each and everyone had sent their love to her. It was ridiculous and lovely to think of the sleeping beauties; any half-awake would lift a soft nose to his hand, hear a name, or be called 'Lassie'. This final check closed the working day well and they usually did it together.

'Now I've made you homesick,' he said, 'tell me what you're up to.' She told him about tackling the journals and how interesting they were but he knew her too well. 'Don't get depressed, the old girl was always cheerful enough.' He was right of course, she was inclined to take things too much to heart. Once on the school bus a friend had described how after an accident a doctor had told the girl to exercise a painful shoulder, insisting this would banish the pain. It did not because the trouble was really a broken collarbone. Getting off at her stop after saying goodbye she had found it difficult to walk home, the pain in her shoulder was so intense. There was a lesson somewhere in that tale.

Chapter 6

The second book was not in the form of a diary. For some reason Aunt Mary had taken up the pen to write of her childhood, of school and teachers, of friends who shared that time. There was no hint of when she decided to go down memory lane or for what reason – the book bore no date, but presumably it was written during wartime. It would be interesting to skim through the pages...

Seeing the snake made a difference to me. I became not brave but adept at hiding what I felt. It happened like this: I was six years old and late for school, not unusually so because my mother was not well and struggled every morning to get me away clean and tidy. I remember scurrying up Grange Road tugging at a coat which didn't sit right on my shoulders and having to stop to fasten shoelaces not properly tied when I was hustled off; the baby had the luck to stay at home. Dealing with the laces was easy when you knew 'left over right, pull quite tight, make a loop do, wind the other over for loop number two'. Then I looked up and saw the Snake. I use a capital letter because even now I can see it arrowing its way to hide among the dark leaves. Rooted like the tree itself I was unable to walk away, fear in my head that the thing might turn, slide towards me... I do not believe I took breath though my heart thumped in my chest: my cold face must have been pale.

I stared up at leaves which had opened like hands for the Snake but Mr Jackson's voice, raised above the chug-chug of his machine, reproached me. 'Nay Mary lass, thy mother sent thee off with time enough. One of Shakespeare's snails thou art. Tha'd best hop in't sidecar!' Stout Mr Jackson, kindness itself I realise now, stopping to scoop me up as a favour to my mother. I remember he sent us lilac in the spring, and other flowers from his garden. Wriggling out of the sidecar, all I had to do was cross the playground without going near the toilet block which even in the morning smelled bad, to find the big door where it said INFANTS above it. How lucky that Miss Robins was coming out of the little room the teachers had for themselves. I really loved Miss Robins: she wore pretty clothes in soft colours but above all, her eyes looked at you as if she knew and liked everything about you.

'Mary! Are you all right love? You're rather late! Never mind. I'll take you in and explain.'

Explain what? She had no idea about the Snake and I dare not speak about it. Hand in hand with Miss Robins in her pale clothes, I was taken to my class teacher Miss Dickson, who was very different. The eyes of Miss Dickson were not dark and kind but pieces of flint as she heard I was not very well yet did not wish to miss school. My dear Miss Robins left with the briefest of smiles and I sat down as ordered. At the same time as Miss Dickson, I saw my shoes were muddied and undone again because of the Snake. When she railed at me for the mess on the floor, there it was, gliding towards me, its tongue flicking in and out... My scream and sobs annoyed my teacher even more.

'You come in late, miss, and so far as I can see there is nothing wrong with you at all. You spread dirt all over my floor and then start bawling like a dying duck in a thunderstorm! I'm not having it, my lady! You'd better go next door, to the babies!' Bad enough, but worse was to come. As I dragged at the door, as often in that draughty old place a gust of wind wrenched it from my hand to crash, breaking its curtain of little coloured beads to send them scooting all over the floor as well as into my mud patch. I did not wait to hear what Miss Dickson said to quieten the class.

I was happier with Miss Robins, helping with the very tiny children. After playtime Mr Gossard, the headmaster, came and peered into the Wendy House where I was reading The Tale of a Turnip to three little ones who were as quiet as mice. Later I was given a note to take to my mother and sent home in the care of Nelly Wright, an older girl who lived next door but one to us. It was awful knowing we had to pass the Snake Tree on the way home and I could not get Nelly to cross soon enough to the other side of the road, so I was tearful again when she handed me over.

My poor mother did not deserve a miserable child. Questioning as she felt my forehead and bathed my face, she settled me on the sofa covered by a blanket brought from upstairs. The horsehair pricked at my bare legs but I was safe at last. I must have slept, but in my dream it was back, slithering so close that my mother had to shake me to stop the noise I made. I almost told but when my eyes cleared and I saw her troubled face I knew it was no good, I could not bother her. I lay for a long time and I believe it was then from within myself came the first glimpse of a hardness to be summoned when there is need.

I endured the rest of my time with Miss Dickson, trying not to be late and giving strict attention to everything she said, and the others called me Teacher's Pet. That was where my new self came in handy to ignore what they said instead of weeping. One day Miss Dickson praised me for reading well and I could hardly believe it when her lips moved in a sort of smile.

When the move came into the big school I was put in the second rather than the first standard and by jumping one class thus lost my tormentors. I worked hard for the new teacher, who treated us all fairly. I remember she had a very nice speaking voice and came from somewhere down South. I learned some fine long words from Miss Sims.

The only drawback now was another Mary in the class, Mary Brooks, the school caretaker's daughter. More or less from *starting school I had paid this girl one halfpenny per week to be left alone, the money collected every Monday morning without fail and if anyone did not pay, the limit was Tuesday dinnertime, or else... The halfpennies bought her sweets every day and not just on Saturday. The caretaker and his wife swept and cleaned the school without knowing about Mary.*

The second week in the big school provided the test for me. 'It'll be a penny, yer missed las' week!' I had a penny given by a neighbour who made me take it though my mother did not like me to be paid for anything done to help people. I saved this penny knowing it would be called for − a bully does not give up. She was big for her age and I had been afraid of her for a long time. I shrank back into the hanging coats but she grabbed me, her rosy face came close and I saw her eyes were green like the snake. That was enough to sting me into action. With all my strength I pushed at her chest, taking her by surprise, off balance, sprawling to the floor and bumping her head. Her mouth opened in a roar so loud it should have brought the whole school at a run, but no one came. I spoke with feeling:

'Yo're nowt but a girt bully an' ahm fed up. Tha's gettin' no more outa me an' that's flat! If tha dun't stoppit ah'll tell, all on 'em ... teacher, yer mum an' dad, an' t'vicar an' all.' I brought the vicar into it because Mr Brooks was a church warden. My victim got up and ran away sobbing. That was it, really. Life went on rather better than before. I made no claim to be the heroine who saved others from blackmail and probably Mary B's teeth in later life. I was merely a worm that turned.

The next day my teacher sent me to Mr Harris, the assistant headmaster, to show him my work. I admired Mr Harris very much, and this is what I wrote − the spelling not so good!

'I like Mr Harris because he is nice and tall. I think Mr Harris is Kind and good. I think Mr Harris would be calm, cool and collected if there was a fire. I beleive he would clear the snakes out of the park on Grange Road.'

Chapter 7

The account of early schooldays continued with another mention of Miss Dickson, then in charge of the class on Mary's first day:

After my dinner I nursed my little brother until my mother said it was time to go back to school. I thought for a minute and then said I wasn't going. 'There in't that much to do, only pot'ooks an' I can do them.' My mother was surprised and said there was much more, learning to read and do sums, I would love all that. I was only half convinced because the real trouble was nothing to do with pothooks so I told the truth: 'It's that teacher,' I said, 'I don't like 'er face!' Plainly this opinion never changed.

One morning my mother pulled back the curtains and said, 'No sun, no moon, no stars, NO-VEMBER!' Everything was blanked out by fog. I had never seen anything like it, a grey cloud lifting just enough to show where Mr Jackson lived but not properly, other houses gone. There was a funny smell which made me cough when I opened the door to let Puss out. I was ready long before Nelly called for me, which she always did now. Then I had a thought, 'Shall I 'ave te grope mi way, with a stick?' After a second or so my mother decided there was no need because Nelly knew what fog was like and if it got too bad we could come back for one. Making sure my coat was fastened, she had a little twitch at the corner of her mouth the same as Mr Harris when he saw my work. The fog wrapped us up. *Thick and yellowish, I could taste it in my throat. Nothing was the same.*

Their feet breaking the silence, her hand in Nelly's, they had edged past the park towards school and the calm of Miss Sims. There a settling process began, a much happier time, with Mary less concerned about leaving her mother, the baby and the cat. Miss Sims had kept an orderly class – '*her eyebrows snapping together in a fierce look but the way she spoke was very clear and different from us*'.

Slowly school became enjoyable; she admired the teacher's Roman nose which stopped her glasses from falling down.

Asked about Miss Sims, I said she was half young and half old but my next teacher was probably only one quarter young. At first I looked very closely at Miss Summers because Nelly's mother said, 'There's a teacher with all her buttons on!' when my mother mentioned the name. I saw the lovely pearl ones on her blouse and cardigan and four shining brass ones on the blazer she wore to school that September when the weather was still warm and had a nice golden look. Miss Summers had a lot of hair with threads of white showing and her face was lined but she had a huge smile when things pleased her. One day someone said, 'I saw Miss Summers at the Queens Hall and she was all in purple, a purple coat, and hat and gloves.' 'And a purple nose!' I added to make people laugh. It was a little bit true about the nose but afterwards I knew I was like Judas Iscariot and should never have said it.

Miss Summers lived with her sister who kept a shop at the corner of the next street but one. I chatted with Mrs Hardisty when I went to spend my Saturday penny after I stopped having to pay Mary Brooks. Mrs Hardisty had a lot of patience when it took time deciding what to get from the halfpenny tray – a creamy Snowball covered with coconut or long strings of liquorice or maybe a gobstopper which lasted for a long time but soon lost its taste. One day I said, 'Do y' knaw what I thowt when I were little?' and she could not think. 'Well,' I said, 'that little thing in yer throat at the back, I imagined food went down one side and drink down t'other!' She looked surprised so I told her more – 'The thing's called thy glottis.' Mrs Hardisty shook her head. 'Nay Mary!' she said. 'You really are a funny little girl!' At the time I did not understand why she said that.

As Christmas drew near a concert was planned to entertain the parents. Mary was dismissive of some of the choices – 'Choral Speaking' and 'Favourite Carols' were too easy, unlike Miss Summers, who was going to do a play. However, lessons were to continue, the real work must go on.

'For some reason Miss Summers did not choose a boy to be Father in the play but gave the part to me and a girl called Edna Thatcher was the Mother. We practised in the afternoons after playtime and decided what to wear. I had cotton shorts with long stockings pulled over the knees like the Prince of Wales when he went to shoot or play golf. Miss Summers asked if anyone would like to sing or recite a poem in the interval between the two parts of our play. I told her about a song I knew. The music had a picture of a little girl in ragged clothes standing near a gas lamp, her poor little feet are bare and she holds out a posy to beautifully dressed ladies who hurry by because it is snowing or they are busy with selfish pleasures. It begins:

> *Underneath the gaslight's glitter*
> *Stands a little flower girl*

then tells about night winds bitter and the girl has not a loving word to cheer her. It ends:

> *There are many, sad and weary*
> *In this pleasant world of ours*
> *Crying in the night so bitter*
> *Won't you buy my pretty flowers?*

I thought this song very tragic and was moved to tears thinking the flowers could not last long in such cold. Miss Summers said I must round up the music, but I had no idea where to look.

How excited we felt, being at school in the dark. We had our tea early as we had to be back there in good time to get ready. The hall was crowded because the concert was free, though on a table at the door was a large sweet jar, probably from Mrs Hardisty's shop, and anyone could put money in that. When the concert began the audience clapped the Choral Speaking and the Favourite Carols and soon it was our turn. The first part went off nicely and then it was the interval. Someone put music on the piano and it was the sad song! No one had mentioned finding it. I needed time to remember the words properly, so I could not go back on the stage to sing, I could not do it. Instead I started to cough and made a splutter into my handkerchief as if I had a sudden cold. I saw Miss Summers tighten her mouth but the audience had to wait. I thought it was for the best, the song might have upset them. The second part of our play began well but we soon lost the thread, not having practised enough. We were unsure and fell into a dreadful silence, shuffled our feet and did not know what to do. I tried to help Miss Summers, who was offstage speaking in a low voice. 'Go on, Edna, it's thy turn...' 'T'int, it's thee...' She would not have it but I knew – 'Say Father's swallered a dicshunnery 'n then...' 'Wrong fer once Cleverdick, allus thinks tha knaws best...' We argued on and got nowhere, unable to

34

hear Miss Summers for the laughing. Before the curtains hid us I could see Nelly's mother, her hands rose and fell as she laughed and laughed.

Miss Summers was quiet with Edna and me the next day but did not grumble at us, said it was water under the bridge and we must all turn to page seventeen of the sum book because some children had not grasped how to do long division and she would go through it again for their sakes.

My mother started early buying extra things so she could make a Christmas cake and Christmas puddings in good time. About the same time as our concert she iced the cake, first with marzipan and then thick white icing, and after it set hard brought out the things we used every year for decoration, a Father Christmas and some little eskimos on sledges. It needed care to put the cake back into the big tin when it was finished. On Christmas Eve I was sent to the shop and to my infinite pleasure Miss Summers was helping her sister as the shop was full. I could not believe my luck when with one of her big smiles she gave me a bar of Cadbury's Dairy Milk and hoped I would have a nice time. Earlier I had told the sisters about last year when there was a tremendous knocking on our front door and my mother sent me to see who it was because she was busy. I opened the door and there was Father Christmas all in red with a sack over his shoulder. Quick as a flash I had shut the door and turned the key on him. Why, I did not know. Both my listeners were amused when I told them it was my uncle who had been to the Oddfellows' party and had enough drink to make him behave oddly. On Christmas Day the presents were useful ones except the baby got a toy. I sometimes got books from my aunt but did not like them much; one was called A Peep Behind the Scenes, *which I never finished. It was nothing like one Nelly showed me, a book called* The Sheik *by Ethel M. Dell about a brave man in a wonderful palace in the middle of a desert. Nelly promised to lend it to me but when she brought it my mother said it was unsuitable and Nelly had to take it home.*

Chapter 8

She knew that as an only child she had been indulged by her father and quite the opposite by a mother whose firm social conscience led her to nag about the good home, nice clothes and prolonged education she had in contrast with children not nearly so lucky. She had felt plagued by those poor children and rudely said, 'Well it's not my fault is it?' or something like that but in the end the talk flowed over her head. She remembered envying the wartime children who did not have to eat vegetables. Now she was given a picture of the young Mary, vulnerable most of all because there was no father and later no mother. In this house the whole came to life, a small girl opening out when the atmosphere was right with kind Miss Robins, Miss Sims and the respected Miss Summers. Home circumstances were not rosy, the mother in poor health, presumably doing without what she could not afford. She remembered her aunt explaining, 'You cut your coat according to the cloth.' The wheels of industry were not kept turning by use of the 'never-never', there was great scorn for that.

Dennis brought happiness and a fair outlook until war changed things for ever. Few means of travel, the villages closing in on themselves, people unable to get about much, needing a torch at night because streetlamps were not lit, the houses blacked out and silent. After a working day and the difficulties of a poorer bus service, finding solace in writing, her aunt had turned to the past, dredging from memory to fill the pages of the little books. One thing was certain: they would not end up in the grate like the other stuff. She was eager to read on; comparing the aunt she knew or thought she knew with child Mary was a revelation. However, first things first: the house neat and tidy, the clip rug asking to be admired, fire glowing, flowers, Sandra helping to set the scene. The agent was coming...

He arrived with his prey, a couple who were middle-aged and had a large car: she could not see them living in the house. Was it another 'buy to let' viewing? The range and the rug were noticed and the brief tour began: the agent doing his best. 'It is a good, solid old house, well taken care of,' she heard, and it was true, her aunt had done what was necessary to keep the place in order without making changes that did not suit. The two coming down the steep stairs had pleasant manners. Subtly younger than her face, the woman's hair was very nice indeed and he had the air of success about him. No coffee required, they thanked her and left. The agent lingered to say another family would like to come the following day if that was all right, and of course it was – had to be because she wanted to go back home. She looked around trying to see what a stranger saw, but could not. For her the place was her aunt, a tiny bit of herself and now the child Mary. She supposed she had been aware this was the family home before the mother died and Mary had gone to live with her aunt Lizzie. When the house became vacant years later, Dennis had secured it for their future home; Mary deciding to stay there alone caused uproar and the anger never abated. Later she made fun of the attempts to dislodge her, but it would have been a difficult situation. A good thing she managed to resist the efforts to get her back, caring for that particular old age less of a burden when Mary was independent and not living under the same roof. Grandma had provided that roof only to treat Mary as a kitchie-deem, a servant for the family, the young men accepting that she was there to wait upon them. Another sort of bereavement came when the brother living in Canada sent only brief replies to her letters and during the war the letters stopped. She had needed the inner core suggested in the tale of the snake.

It was good to get back to the next chapters, which moved on to Mr Harris, the admired assistant headmaster. An adult eye could see the child innocently and beautifully under a spell, and Mr Harris as a worthy man.

When Miss Summers chose me as her monitor I was sent many times to Mr Harris's classroom because she needed pencils, notebooks, or any of the school things kept in his cupboards. Mr Harris would breathe in and break off talking to his children to give me the stuff with a weary little smile. Mr Harris was handsome enough to be a film star; something made you keep looking when his eyes twinkled down at you. I did not change my mind about him.

The oldest girls used to get a heavy rope from the teachers' room and chant different rhymes as they skipped smartly in and out as the rope swung. One of the rhymes was about Mr Harris.

Mr Harris is a very good man
He tries to teach us all he can
Reading, writing, arithmetic
But he never forgets to
Give us the stick.

and

Mr Harris is a very good man
He goes to church on Sundays
To pray to God to give him strength
To cane us all on Mondays.
When he does he makes us dance
Out of England into France
Out of France and into Spain
Then over the hills and back again.

The words came drifting across to the Infants' space and into your mind, then suddenly you were an older girl, skipping away, panting out the words and hoping you would not be the one to break the rhythm. When I reached his class I made certain never to deserve the stick Mr Harris kept on top of his cupboard. He did not use it much but made the naughtiest boys think he would if they did not change.

'A good thrashing is it thou'rt wanting Willie Metcalf?' Or John Ledgard, or Alan Barr ... the cane tapping the desk, eyes almost closed to shut out the wickedness... 'For thee lad, one more chance, one ... CHANCE!...' The cane whistling down would make me and the other girls jump out of our skins, but boys pretended not to care or scowled at their hands. If the worst happened the boy blew on his palms or muttered to us, 'Din't 'urt!' but quick to say 'No sir' if Mr Harris asked did he want another one?

I sat at the back of the room and my partner in the double desk was a clever boy called Sidney Seaman. At first I did not like him because his clothes smelled, but after a while I got used to how it was and liked Sidney for himself. In fact, we chatted so much that Mr Harris moved him and put Alan Barr in his place. None of us were smart but our mothers sewed or knitted things and mended torn clothes, but Sidney's mother did not believe that 'soap and water cost nowt', as they did, and never bothered washing or darning his clothes. She did not bake bread or cakes either. He was unlucky really.

40

As Christmas drew near people seemed disappointed we were not planning to do a play and asked kindly after Edna Thatcher. Like Miss Summers, our teacher thought school work had to come first, and only at the last minute did he say the boys' choir had learned some special Christmas songs and we would all be on the stage with the choir at the front: Sidney Seaman would begin 'Once in Royal David's City' and we would join in. I began to worry about Sidney's clothes but it turned out that Mr Harris had arranged with the vicar to borrow the church choirboys' things which Mrs Harris was going to wash and iron before sending them back in time for Sunday.

At rehearsal a few of the boys misbehaved, pushing each other, pretending they had not enough room and might fall off the stage. Mr Harris put a stop to that, threatening to tear Willie Metcalf limb from limb if it happened on the night. Our part in the concert went very well, Sidney's voice so sweet and clear that everybody listened, and we sang nicely too.

After the concert the only thing left for us was the Christmas party. Not a great deal of fuss was made, but at about two o'clock tea was laid on trestle tables in the hall and when that was cleared away we were to have games until hometime. It was a surprise to see a girl who had just come to the school wearing a very fancy frock and we were all staring at her as we queued for places at the table. Stepping out of line she fluffed the skirt, gave a twirl and sank into a curtsey, a butterfly before a crowd of very dull moths, the female ones downcast. This was not lost on Miss Summers. 'Yvonne, is it? Looking for a partner, are you dear? Have Tommy!' Like Sidney in not having much truck with soap and water, Tommy was more than willing to be nudged forward. Now the butterfly's face crumpled but Miss Summers was firm. 'Look after our new *girl, Tommy. Stay with her ... at the end of the line there.' A radiant Tommy obeyed. I saw Mr Harris give Miss Summers one of his best smiles as she turned away.*

Chapter 9

The writing continued:

When springtime came my mother sometimes walked up Grange Road to meet me coming from school, wheeling the pushchair along in case the baby's fat little legs got tired. At the same time of day Mrs Harris might decide to bring her baby to meet my teacher. I was pleased but embarrassed if they arrived together, afraid my mother might tell some of the things I said about Mr Harris. She thought Mrs Harris a very nice young woman with a sweetly pretty face and a right bonny head of hair, and the baby looked just like her. I could not agree. Seeing the baby's eyes half closed as she lay back against a pillow she seemed to me the spitten image of Mr Harris, but I kept quiet about it. They lived in a newly built house beyond our road and he passed our house on the way to school. I never dared to catch him up; to walk with the teacher would be just too much, though he turned to say Good Morning if I was tagging along on the far side of the road well away from the park.

At about this time an older girl called Amy, who was a friend of Nelly's, asked Nelly and me to tea in one of the new houses. I was very impressed by everything so fresh and different but was completely floored when Amy told us that often she went over to take the baby for a walk while Mrs Harris did housework or anything else.

'You tek it for walks, on't cinder path or the Rec?'

''Course I do, anywhere I want.' 'Do ye' ... I could hardly

spit it out, 'd'ye go in...?' "Course I do!' She and Nelly were looking at each other so I didn't say any more. I peered across to the house with a blue door and a white fence round the garden. Mr Harris had tulips and wallflowers and a little bush with pretty yellow flowers all in bloom. It was lovely. 'Thank you very much indeed,' I said to Amy's mother and ran home to think about everything.

My mother said that there was nothing to stop me taking my little brother down the cinder path any time I wanted, as long as I really looked after him and didn't forget he was with me. Once when I found a wild flower I had never seen before I ran home with it, leaving him crawling about the meadow, and she had come running back with me in a panic. I did not like being reminded of this and thought it better to watch for Amy and the pram without the extra responsibility.

When I went down the cinder path with Amy and the dear little baby I told her about leaving my brother in the meadow, expecting her to laugh, but she said, 'If I told Mrs Harris that, you'd never get near this pram!' so I could have bitten my tongue off. Amy was generally disappointing to me, she could not remember anything about the furniture in Mrs Harris's house. 'You seem real nosey to me,' she said, and I was hurt because it wasn't like that. I decided Nelly was nicer than Amy; old friends were best. I did learn from Amy though. Speaking about another village, when I asked, 'Is there any shops?' she puckered her mouth and answered, 'Yes, there ARE shops.' I seldom made that mistake again.

It seemed to be a good time for learning. Mr Harris had a way of putting things very clearly and often made little jokes which made you remember what he was telling you. He was clever at inventing short cuts in arithmetic: a nought on the end if you multiply by ten; by nine do the same and take whatever number it is away from the total. Another thing was

44

factorise, always factorise. I made a solemn vow never to forget it.

My mother needed medicine when my little brother became ill and because the chemist did not open until nine o'clock, rather than keep me from school she sent me to get my mark in the register, but with a note asking if I could go out to the chemist: I could then take the medicine home with me at twelve o'clock. I was nervous about this, sensing the headmaster might not like the idea, and I approached timidly after the morning prayers. It seemed to take an age for everybody to march back to class roughly in time to music played on the piano. Mr Gossard frowned when he read the note and looked at me over his glasses. 'I can't let you out of school for this!' he said. 'Is there nobody else who could go?'

'No sir,' I quavered. 'Mi mother can't. I'm forced to!' ...

A long pause, then with some irritation, 'Very well. Be as quick as you can. Look both ways when you cross!'

I was so relieved I tried to lighten things up with a joke. 'T'ud be a job if t'chemist dint open up today!'

Mr Gossard stared, and then he thundered, 'He WILL be open! STUPID child!'

The teacher closing up the piano, the stragglers late for school, the caretaker coming in to sweep and the class settling for lessons at the far end of the hall all heard. They heard 'WI...LL' and 'STU...PID' bounce and shudder from ceiling and walls as I slunk to the door, my heart like a stone. I wept as I flew through the school gate and across the road to the chemist's. Norman, the kind assistant there, said, 'Nay Mary lass, thy brother's not goin' te dee, it's nobbut a bit of a cowd he's got!'

I snuffled through the rest of the morning; even Mr Harris could not get a smile out of me, it was so horrible being stupid and everybody knowing it except me. I hoped my mother would not find out what Mr Gossard thought of me on top of all her

45

worries. That was the only time I was ever unhappy in Mr Harris's class and strangely enough after I got back from the errand it began to rain and never stopped, just like me! Even now I dislike remembering the SHOU...OU...T.

Summer came early and in no time at all the trees were fully out. In Grangefield Park it was impossible to see through the thick green leaves, anything could be hiding there...

A note is added at a later date:

That was the year of the scholarship exam but nothing much was made of it; people thought, if you pass, well and good. If not, you leave school, get a job and earn some money. Locally for boys the jobs were at Dawson, Payne & Elliot, Bremner, Waite & Savile, firms with a worldwide reputation for making printing machines. There were woollen, silk and paper mills, electrical engineers, tanneries, glass-blowing at Guiseley, openings of many sorts and apprenticeships for some trades. For a girl, passing for the grammar school was considered a waste as she would most likely get married.

Not everyone went in for the scholarship, only those who worked hard enough, just a few from our class. One Saturday morning my mother gave me threepence return fare and I went to wait at Iron Row for a bus to Ilkley: I had to ask the conductor to stop the bus near the school where the exam was held. I worried a bit about the bus being late, and then about the conductor remembering the right place. I walked along and to my relief saw the school. Our desks were well away from each other so there could be no copying. Who, of all people, was in charge of the examination? Mr Harris! It made me and the others feel really at home and we got down to answering the papers. I remembered not to be like Tommy Tregennis in one of my books, so clever he spent all his time thinking of exactly the right word to use and had to give in a blank sheet of paper at the end. Mind you, with Mr Harris there I did forget it was an exam and, puzzling over a choice of words, I looked up and said, 'Sir, which d'y'think's best...' a bit like Tommy Tregennis after all. However, before I finished the question, Mr Harris shook his head and put his finger to his lips, trying not to smile.

Chapter 10

I became friendly with Edna Thatcher and was allowed to go with her to a special meeting held in the early evening in the Wesleyan School. We found it strange going into another school though it had the same kind of smell and the same painted brick walls, the main difference being stairs to a second floor. Making a careful way up stone steps I had a thought: 'I reckon they'll rush up an' down an' teachers'll shout!' Edna knew something: 'Wesleybugs is a reet rough lot!' Giggling at the rough Wesleybugs, we found an open door and were welcomed by grown-ups whose smiles stayed as other children came in and walked to rows of desks, each one higher than the last to make it easy to see the blackboard. One of the ladies went to a piano and played some jolly hymns. During the singing a few boys were acting about but Edna and I sang as well as possible without a hymn book. After that a tall thin man told us about a family whose father spent all their money on drink so they had bare feet even in winter and not enough food to keep healthy. Edna and I were thankful our homes were not like that. More glad hymns and another story and then it was the end but a lady said would anybody care to sign up to become a Little White Ribboner and never allow strong drink to touch our lips. The boys went off but we joined the queue and were smiled at again. We had really enjoyed ourselves. I planned to write about it next day. At home I tried to drink my milk without it touching my lips and it was not at all easy. We were promised a White Ribbon to wear but this never came and we stopped going to the meetings.

* * *

48

Nice weather brought walks in the lanes and through the fields, or sometimes down by the river, always with Nelly or Edna, or mothers and babies when there was a path for the pushchairs. A neighbour got engaged and cleared out some of her belongings, giving me her bicycle and a red and white scarf. Her young man mended punctures and altered the height of the saddle. I was delighted with such a generous gift.

I decided to wear the scarf tied at the back in a smart way and rode off into the sunshine where, at the bottom of Back Lane, I found Edna and two more girls and of all people Mary Brooks. I saw them looking at my bike and leaned over to hide the handlebars which needed rubber grips on the ends. Mary Brooks said, 'Yon bike's seen better days, that owd saddle must 'urt yer bum!' I could see Edna did not care for the rude word but she said nothing. A girl called Elsie leaned forward and tugged at my scarf, 'Thinks she's posh! Goin' to t'Grammer!'

I rode off to the Rec and went round a few times before going home. My mother was resting so I climbed on a chair to look in the mirror. I had to see what I looked like. I stared at a round face with the scarf slipping to one side now. I took it off. Hair between light and dark, eyes not to my liking as I would have preferred blue not greyish and my eyebrows were too strong. I really hated it if Alan Barr called me 'Saucer-ees' when we fell out. My nose was just a nose; teeth white enough but not quite straight. When Nelly put lipstick on us both it felt nice but you were supposed to have a Cupid's bow shape. In Nelly's magazine the film stars were beautiful Claudette Colbert had an unusual face, Janet Gaynor looked almost like an ordinary person. Jean Harlow had very white hair but the most important was Marlene Dietrich. Once, before Nelly got too old for me, she sucked in her cheeks and said, 'Guess who?' meaning Marlene. I tried that but the mirror told me I looked daft. It was depressing not to be beautiful: I could not possibly be posh either, on that old bike.

Mary's last summer at the village school was carefully written up, with Mr Harris shown to have serious troubles and Mary quite devastated by the discovery. The eventful day had started off happily, the observations perceptive as ever. A clear picture emerges of a village where the school has an important place in the community, people are interested and happy to give support. The village recreation ground was always known as the 'Rec'. In Mary's eyes, the spelling should have been 'wreck' as everything in the place at that time was broken or nearly so. The see-saw could be made to work if more children sat at one end than the other, and the wood splintered so children got 'spells' in bare legs. Swings had seats hanging loose or missing altogether. One piece of equipment boys played on but the iron bars were too stiff for small girls. A tall frame had ropes with rings, but these were knotted out of reach by youths using them for acrobatics. A path went round the whole of the Rec and anyone with a bike could speed round looking out for clumps of grass springing up through the cracked concrete. A maypole was useable though most of the ropes were without padding at the end and the concrete round it was in a rough state. The shelter had only one or two good seats but Mary and her friends played at houses there and ignored the broken places.

It must have been fine in the beginning with lots of fancy woodwork and mothers could have chosen to sit whichever side the sun happened to be. Sometimes I tried to think of the Rec when everything was new, with a ribbon tied across the gates on the very first day and an important person cutting it to let them swing open for all the boys and girls to rush in to the different things. I had seen a book called Children's Games *with pictures of little girls in old-fashioned long dresses in pretty pale colours: I imagined the skirts like flower bells as they went spinning round the maypole, every rope in use. A sight for sore eyes, I thought.*

Besides playing houses, the Rec was a good place for skipping and for singing games like the ones in the book when enough children turned up to make it worthwhile. A girl called Susan Parker who lived in a row of houses just outside the Rec gates would start us off with 'Jolly Miller' or 'London Bridge' and we had other favourites such as 'There came Three Dukes a-Riding' or 'Oats and Beans'. I was always chosen first if we did 'Poor Mary sat a-weeping'.

Some mothers were not keen on Susan Parker, who was a very adventurous girl with a lot of brothers. Nelly said Mrs Parker always wanted a little girl but when Susan got into even worse scrapes than the boys Mrs Parker wondered why she bothered. I heard that Susan climbed out of an attic window in their roof to sit on the slates and hold long conversations with her best friend Moira who leaned from a window in her house across the way. I admired Susan for doing this because I never would have dared, the very thought made me dizzy. Both girls went to the Wesleyan School but I did not mention Wesleybugs to them. I asked if they ever went to the Little White Ribboners but they had never heard of it. Susan said anyway she often took strong drink because her uncle was in the Royal Navy and let her have some of his rum when he came on leave. Nelly said 'Fat chance! At twelve an' six a bottle he'd never waste it on a little kid!' They often argued.

After the Council made hay from the long grass, we had the school sports day in the Rec. The school caretaker marked out lines for running races with a little machine borrowed from the Cricket Club; I expect Mr Harris thought of that. We prayed for fine weather and wanted as many people as possible to come and watch us.

The day came with never a cloud in the sky and the promise of heat, so most of the village turned out. It would be a perfect day for having a chat in the sunshine and catching up with news you might have missed. The long crocodile of excited children had marched down Main Street managing to behave, some under threat, Mr Gossard careful of the school's good name. Mr Harris of course kept perfect control with the worst offenders close to him as Mary noticed.

After taking part the children were allowed to join their parents or friends, but were under strict orders not to leave the Rec.

I had on my new yellow dress made as a present for passing the exam. I saw my mother and Nelly's mother and Mrs Hardisty arrive, she must have closed the shop. A lot of people came together from the new houses, and amongst them Mrs Harris in the prettiest blue dress, looking happy wheeling the pram. Mr Harris of course was too busy to notice, having to organise the whole thing and tell the teachers what to do. Disappointing most girls in our class, their baby was christened Jane: we had hoped for something better, like Claudette or Jeanette or Madeline after film stars; some fancied Marina, others Rebecca. I really liked Bryony taken from a story I read but they said it was silly, she would end up as Bryan. I used to have a doll I called May Blossom and Nelly's little cousin called hers Violet Gum but kept quiet about that. We all agreed Jane was altogether too plain for such a beautiful child. The afternoon got hotter and running races was very tiring. I could not get my legs going fast enough to win, but Nelly ended up as Champion of the Seniors. The Junior champion turned out to be Mary Brooks, a great surprise. The champions each got a box of Black Magic and Nelly said she would share hers when we got home. Mary Brooks said she must be daft. We were looking for our mothers when something terrible happened so quickly we stood there stupidly, mouths open, unable to understand why suddenly Mrs Harris had fallen to the ground, shuddering and kicking and rolling about, grass staining the pretty dress, a high heel broken off. Someone wheeled the baby out of the way. Mr Harris came at a run and knelt, forcing something into her mouth. People crowded round and Mr Harris said 'Move back' in a strange voice. I could not bear to see any more and ran at full tilt not really knowing where I was going. Coming to the maypole I grabbed a rope and ran round and round before lifting my legs to swing wildly through the air. Of course I had forgotten to put my hands high up on the rope and when the rotten padding gave way, I fell on the rough concrete.

Back at home on the sofa, the horsehair pricking only where my legs were not bandaged, I stopped crying but still felt very bad. My mother said the blood was soaking out of the dress and I hadn't to worry; even if it didn't it wasn't the end of the world. She kept looking at me as if she knew there was something else and of course there was: it was poor Mrs Harris so strange and ill and the baby wheeled away from her. It was Mr Harris, his face so sad ...

Bleak midwinter in spite of the sunshine. Poor Mary. The snakes still there, a white fence had not kept them out.

Chapter 11

From the closely written pages came hardly a hint of the aunt she had confided in rather than her mother, the cheerful woman whose letters to her breathed common sense during her first taste of independence. More real was the blossoming child always vulnerable, aware of the misfortunes of others. Often the words reflected that child rather than the woman writing them. Eleven-year-old Mary is speaking:

It came, the day I dreaded. When my mother told me that in no time at all I would love the new school and the teachers there would be just as nice as the ones I knew, it was her way of cheering me up: I knew full well there would not be another Miss Summers and how could there possibly be anyone like Mr Harris? I thought grammar school teachers might be too busy to care about you in the same way when the school was huge with hundreds and hundreds of pupils. However, I knew I had to put up with it and be of good cheer. Mr Palmer-Paterson, our vicar, often mentioned that.

My mother called me early knowing I had so much on my mind I would be anxious not to be late. She liked to say what the weather was like and when it was a horrible day tried to make it sound better. 'I've warmed the earth for you,' she would say on a bitter winter morning to make getting out of bed nicer. I was early enough to spend a little time brushing my dear cat thinking I could be busy with homework later on. She was such a lovely creature it was a pleasure to take care of her. How I was going to find time for my friends I did not know, but I would never neglect my cat.

When I put on the square-neck blouse and gymslip I felt strange. A long mirror would have been useful. Climbing up on the old dresser I could not get a proper look; my impression was it did not suit a straight up-and-down shape, the stiff blue girdle would have to be pulled tight if I wanted a waist, but I left it alone for the time being. My mother wanted me to eat a cooked breakfast on this first day but even a piece of toast tasted like cardboard and stuck in my throat so I drank the tea too hot and burned my mouth. It was still far from the time we had planned I should set off to catch a school bus coming from Ilkley. Ready on the table was my bus pass and dinner money and also three shillings and sixpence for a school hat with the badge at the front. I put on my navy nap coat and my mother decided I had better wear my beret so as not to be a drowned rat if it rained. In spite of the joke I thought she looked a little bit sad and I turned lots of times to wave at her standing with my little brother at the gate.

I cannot say my heart was a stone as I walked away but I think a mournful streak was uppermost. In spite of the day having a nice golden light and the trees turning a nice colour, I longed to forget my new school and follow the old route to dear Mr Harris and my usual classmates, even the rough boys like Willie Metcalfe. As well as saying be of good cheer, Mr Palmer-Paterson reminded us to lift up our eyes unto the hills, but as I was walking fast and a long way from the moors that was no good to me.

My main thought was to get to the bus stop, no matter how long I had to wait there. George from the butcher's was outside the shop talking to the postman. 'What's thy 'urry?' he shouted, 'Is theear a fire or summat?' And they both laughed. I felt my cheeks go red but did not stick my nose into the air, wary of what people said about going to the 'grammer'. No one else was waiting for the bus so I just stood there trying to look bored, but after a while more children arrived, including a girl I knew but did not care for. At last the red bus came and we got on to find most seats taken. I had to sit near a complete stranger who took a good look at me and said, 'I'm Bunty,' a new name to me. I said my name. She was friendly and told me about Switzerland where she had spent ten whole days on holiday for the cost of five pounds. Only once in my life had I seen a crinkly white five-pound note but I guessed that was good value for money. I could not think of anything to say about abroad so Bunty talked to two girls on the seat in front. It was then across the gangway I noticed a lady with a brown face and very yellow hair. I could see long legs in black stockings and she was wearing a gymslip under a long black coat. Someone asked this lady about her holiday and when asked the same thing back, the girl said, 'Yes, maarvlus thanks Miss Peters,' not in a Yorkshire voice but at least I learned the teacher's name.

The bus rattled along the narrow road towards Otley. Animals grazing the fields on either side did not bother to look up. Past Otley Mill and long rows of houses, the printing machine works, shops of all kinds and a cinema, and then a policeman on traffic duty held up a white-gloved hand for us to stop. After a turn left and left again we had to slow down a lot for the old bridge across the river. A man was feeding the swans and plenty of boats were tied up for anyone who wanted to go rowing. I saw a nice bowling green for old people. One more turning and then a jerky stop outside the school. Some girls pushed and scrambled to get out quickly, but not those near Miss Peters. I thought they had better manners and did the same, being one of the last. The bus journey over, I followed the crowd through some fine gates to start my new life.

At the end of the page a note read:

I could not find out where to buy the cap with the badge so

had to wear the beret next day when it was raining heavily. Unfortunately the colour ran so I was a drowned rat after all with red streaks down my face and neck. I had to think it would have been worse if the new cap had got the drenching.

Chapter 12

One viewer on the horizon, an appointment at the weekend which the agent promised might lead to something, but she had begun to think that he would never get anyone to buy the little house. To Sandra she said, 'Maybe he should change the aftershave,' but Sandra understood the joke was to cover how much she wanted him to get a move on so she could get back home.

'It's the nicest house in all the row,' she said, 'just needs the right sort to see it,' and then invited her to supper next door, making a pleasant change.

She had wondered in the early days of meeting Sandra about her not being married and about two children there sometimes and at other times not, but now she was on good terms with Darren, the boyfriend or 'bidey-een' as they would say at home. The two children were Sandra's and now and again they spent time with their father in his new household. It was all very simple in the modern way. Perhaps due to Sandra's inherent good sense, things had sorted themselves out and the folks living next door made a nice family. Supper was a meal served without fuss, the children and Darren at ease with each other, Sandra firm about table manners, insisting on 'Please may I leave the table?' which was old-fashioned and nice.

At home again she went back to the writings. She had been looking forward to the first impressions of the 'Grammer' but there was little. Had her aunt tired of recording, doubted the value of it, or simply found something more interesting to occupy her time? There was no telling. Almost a year elapsed before the following:

I was invited to a party given by a teacher who was leaving to be married, and to my surprise and pleasure it was to take place at Burley. We all piled into a tiny little bus and Miss Bouch drove it, which was unexpected and a little bit alarming when we made a jumpy start. Soon we reached Iron Row and I looked about hoping I would see someone to wave at but there was no one. We went down Iron Row, past the Mill and down the road beside the Goit. I hoped Miss Bouch would drive carefully as it was quite narrow and not used much except by people walking. However, we got to the Dam Stones with no trouble and all got out and waited for Miss Bouch to park the bus: she had to go along the road to leave it in front of some old houses there.

There was a lovely picnic place on the far bank of the river but you had to cross by means of the stepping stones. In winter the water swirled through, completely covering some of them. The worry of that stayed at the back of my mind until I saw the water was gentle and slow and we managed nicely. Miss Bouch and the other teacher with us took great care, not wanting anybody to fall in of course. It felt good once you were safely across, though it would have been unwise to try the same thing in winter. That day the weather was perfect and as soon as Miss Bouch chose the place for the picnic we set about eating all the things she provided – sandwiches, buns and iced cakes, with lemonade to drink. The teachers kept making us eat more until we were all ready to burst. Next came the idea of games, the boys kicking a ball about and some girls playing rounders. Miss Jones joined in the football and Miss Bouch organised the rounders but left them to it and came over to where Peggy Rayner and I were lying in the shade. It was so lovely watching insects skimming the surface of the little pools at the river's edge and we saw two sparrows having a bath, splashing and fluttering their wings and hopping in and out.

'Lazybones!' said Miss Bouch. 'I bet you are too fat to jump the beck!' and offered to race us to see who got there first. That certainly was not me. After a lot of jumps we sat down again and Miss Bouch pointed to the boys who still had their pullovers on, saying it was an odd thing that in winter boys always went out to play in shirtsleeves and had to be sent back in to get their coats. We agreed that it was strange.

That day of the picnic we saw a new Miss Bouch looking very nice in a bright dress different from her school clothes and not wearing her reading glasses. Her face seemed lighted up from inside, and we sensed how happy she was. Before that day we all thought it a pity that Miss Bouch was leaving to be married as her husband would have to be fairly old and need a lot of looking after. I guessed she probably wanted to be a bride, Nelly said everyone did.

When I got back home I was rather quiet and my mother asked was I tired. In fact I was thinking of Miss Bouch looking so pretty in her new clothes. The man she was going to marry had come to take her home in his car, leaving Miss Jones to drive the bus. He was not at all old, but a fine figure of a man and he looked rich. He chatted to Miss Jones with his arm round Miss Bouch's shoulders and I saw him give her a little squeeze. I truly did not want to say goodbye to Miss Bouch, I would miss the way she spoke and was so nice. One thing I decided to keep to myself about the happy day – when Miss Bouch tried to do a double-somersault I caught a glimpse of her knickers, navy blue they were, just like mine.

When the summer holiday arrived Mary was surprised to be given holiday tasks, to read *Ivanhoe* by Sir Walter Scott and to write an essay on a subject of her choice. She chose to write about the cinema but, having very little experience at the time as funds did not run to the weekly trips enjoyed by some of her friends, she relied on what they told her and to the earlier knowledge of her mother and anyone she came across.

I got a good mark for writing about the pictures, Miss Boden said I had done well to find out about very early films she had not been lucky enough to see. I got a scolding for the Ivanhoe *because I never settled to read it from the battered old copy I found and the story was not to my liking anyway. With* Ivanhoe *I used my imagination and must have got it wrong. Writing about the pictures was different, though I did leave out one which gave me nightmares when I was very young. I never liked thinking about the witch in the film; she had a horrible face and with bare hands plucked flaming coals out of the fire to throw at people, chanting something about blood. She was really nasty and for a while I could not forget her. She always came into mind when in icy weather my mother used to take a shovelful of coal from the downstairs fire to warm our bedroom. I remember following after her, the stairway different from in daytime with huge shadows flickering as they sidled past, enough to torment me and confuse her into dropping the shovel. But then we would reach the landing safely and my mother would shovel the coals into the grate, light the gas with a taper and go back downstairs to get my little brother.*

I wrote for Miss Boden about seeing a Cowboy and Indians film which was so exciting that a boy tried to warn the cowboys by yelling out, 'Eh up! One's theer, be'int tree!' and all the people in the Queens Hall laughed. Serial films were shown every week and my friends said they could hardly wait to see what would happen, but I did not get to see them so could not judge. Another film I saw when I was very young affected me strongly so I wrote about that in the homework. It was about a man with a beard and dirty clothes who owned a farm, not a real farm but a place where babies no one wanted were kept in cots stacked one above the other all round the room. The place was isolated and surrounded by dark woods, almost a jungle, hard to get through. The man kidnapped an orphan girl and dragged her to the farm to look after the babies and other children while he went off, usually to collect letters with money sent by people who did not know what an awful man he was, caring only for the money: he kept that and threw the letters into a swamp. He managed to get more and more orphans and needed further help and this time it was a slender girl with a delicate pale face – it was Mary Pickford! She soon made a great improvement, cooking and cleaning and washing everything, and the children and babies became happier. However, they had to hide this from the horrible man and pretend to be just as bad as before, because Mary Pickford was planning to escape, taking all the orphans with her. One night she did just that, leading them through the dark wood in their night clothes, some carrying babies, Mary herself taking the newest one. They had a hard time of it with disaster never far away and worse to come when they heard the man crashing through the wood after them. Luckily he had forgotten about the swamp and fell in. I have never forgotten how dreadful it was watching him sink down and down until only his fingertips were showing … and then nothing!

I was very relieved for Mary and all the children and babies but afterwards kept remembering the swamp and the wicked man's terrible fate. When I was writing the essay I asked my mother about it, thinking of Mr Palmer-Paterson and our Christian duty. She said, 'Don't forget it was only a film and the actor probably never went near a swamp, they have clever ways of doing things in Hollywood.'

Chapter 13

Possibly writing of the holiday essay for Miss Boden triggered the information on cinema-going in the next pages:

Films were mostly made in Hollywood with only an occasional one from Britain. Actors went to Hollywood to become really well-known. If you missed a film at your local cinema it would be there the following week in another place not far away. From the village, keeping up to date with the latest films meant a journey of a few miles on a West Yorkshire red bus or a Ledgard's blue one. If you were lucky enough to get one of the infrequent ones servicing York or Harrogate the ride was more comfortable. In earlier days, no matter how long they had waited at the bus stop, everyone dreaded to see a certain bus approach: the 'Yellow Peril' was a boneshaker, often breaking down on a hill and sometimes people had to ask the driver to stop while they got out to be sick, or so I was told.

With two cinemas in one small town and three in another it was interesting to think you could see so many films. It did not matter to us of course, but Monday, Tuesday and Wednesday saw the first offering with a matinee on Wednesday afternoon. The programme changed for Thursday, Friday and Saturday, with Saturday having a matinee and two evening sessions. At one time you could get a seat for threepence but this no longer applied; the cheapest seats were sixpence and then ninepence, one shilling, one and sixpence, and dearer still the half-crowns. At a newly built picture house in Ilkley there was the added attraction of a cinema organ which rose from some mysterious source when in an interval lights were switched on and girls walked around with trays of ice cream or sweets and chocolate.

Child Mary takes over the next pages:

I went to the New Cinema on my birthday and enjoyed the films and the interval when the organist played brilliantly I thought; his plump little fingers went over the keys so fast you could hardly see them. When he played some tunes the music appeared on the screen with the words underneath and a little while ball bounced from one note to another so everyone knew what to sing. I liked that. Some time afterwards Nelly told me the organist had got the sack and a lady took his place. Thin, Nelly said she was, and a bit miserable though she smiled and waved going down with the organ. Much later I heard my mother and Mrs Wright talking as they looked at the evening paper.

'How sad!' my mother said, shaking her head. 'A real musician like that!'

'He won't be giving 'em "Roses of Picardy" in Armley jail,' said Nelly's mum, 'his favourite, they say.'

I had to ask ... 'Who's gone to jail? Not...'

I said the name of the jolly organist and they both looked uncomfortable so I knew it was. I persisted, 'Why? What's 'e done?'

Mrs Wright was exasperated. 'Of course Miss Big Ears must put a spoke in!'

My mother said quietly, 'Go and find Nelly, love, we're talking about things you wouldn't understand.'

I went, but not without a parting shot ... 'I might! If I got t'chance.'

Once when we were telling secrets to one another Edna Thatcher confessed she was afraid of the dark and hated it in winter when the darkness lasted so long. That reminded me of being afraid about a song which went like this:

Are you there, Mr Bear?
Don't you dare to take a bite off me,
For I shall scream and very quick
My papa will fetch a stick,
And he's not afraid of bears, not he!
So if you want a little baby girl
and you're hungry and you can't wait any more,
I can tell you where there's plenty,
Go and try at Number Twenty.
Go and bite the little girl next door!

I explained I was very small then and worried about the bear and did not want it to go to Nelly's house either. When I went up to bed I used to remember the song and then try to get it out of my mind. Edna had told her mother about being frightened of the dark and Mrs Thatcher said 'When it happens, say "Friends, protect me!" and everything will be all right.'

Mrs Thatcher went to the Spiritualist meetings, though Mr Thatcher said it was a load of nonsense. I did not know what to think but it did give me an idea. Hanging above the fireplace in our bedroom was a picture of a man in old-fashioned clothes, with two collie dogs at his side. I believe he was a shepherd taking a little rest on the moors somewhere, though his sheep were not in the picture. I spent time staring at the scene because it was so peaceful and the man had such a kind face; the dogs had beautiful faces too. Darkness or shadows on the wall as I went to bed used to make me remember things like the bear or the witch, the poor orphans and the man in the swamp when I was really young, and then later I got to worrying about leaving dear Mr Harris and never finding friends in a big school and having homework to do. I realised it was no good being like that and I had to change. I decided that if all the worries started up the best plan was to think of the shepherd, imagine him on the tops in the early-morning sunshine, his dogs ranging far and wide over the heather to round up the sheep. In a way he was like the Good Shepherd mentioned by Mr Palmer-Paterson in church and I found him helpful.

The only time this failed to work was when something really frightening happened, of all places on the moors not far away. Everybody loved walking on the moors, the air so different with all the scents of grass and heather and bilberries coming together and the yellow gorse to dazzle your eyes. The sheep were so used to people they did not bother to run away as you climbed the stony paths. Often little birds rose up together, going high into the sky and then came back almost to the same place. You could hear the chuckling noise of grouse but they kept well out of sight. If you worked in a factory or a mill with the clatter of machinery in your ears you would long to get on the bus and go to the moors at weekends. Then suddenly nobody wanted to go on the walks because of the happening, a murder. Again, people stopped talking if you seemed to be listening but I read the newspaper and knew about it: A young woman was discovered lying on the moor, her life taken away. It was the first time in living memory that such a terrible thing happened there they said, particularly to someone from a good home. There was a lot of whispering from people but I relied on Nelly for information and also from a girl who lived on Station Road. Margaret Horsfall said the police knew exactly who killed the poor lady but I would not have it: 'If they knew 'e'd be in prison by now!'

She looked pityingly at me and with a little smirk said, 'Ah! They can't prove it but my uncle's a policeman himself and he says they'll watch this man day and night and if he puts a foot wrong, they'll have 'im!'

This made me shiver. Being watched day and night and if you made the smallest mistake they would pounce... 'That 'ud be...'

66

Another girl tried to help.

'Mary's not on his side, she's only...'

Margaret was scornful, 'She'd better think of that poor woman!'

I was close to weeping. 'I am, I am,' I gulped, and it was true. We were on the bus on the way home from school yet I was on the moors with the bubbly sound of the beck in my ears, the grass cropped so it was slippery to walk on and the tiny birds swooping down and all the scents so lovely you never forgot... Yes, I did think of the poor lady who could not smell or see or hear because she was dead and I wished with all my heart it had never happened.

Chapter 14

Even as a child I was not happy at Aunt Lizzie's though the house was big and quite interesting with rooms I would have liked to spend time in, but never did as she would quickly call me back to her side as she cooked something for my uncle and the two cousins who lived at home. Her kitchen range had to be blackleaded each week, early in the morning before a fire was lighted. Everybody had that sort of kitchen except people in new houses like Amy and her family and it must have been lovely for the mother not to have to do such a dirty job, though I suppose a handy kind of father might have taken it on. When the blacklead was rubbed off and the steel bits buffed up it looked really nice and there was room for a fine big fire. An oven was on one side of the fire and a boiler for hot water on the other; you scooped the water out with a lading can and carried it to the scullery sink. An oven could get red hot or be slow and tiresome if the coal was of poor quality or damp for some reason. Good coal made a difference with such a lot of baking to do for a family; it was awful in really bad weather when the roads were difficult for a horse and cart and your coal was almost finished. My mother used to give the coalmen large mugs of tea and pieces of teacake. I found the mugs difficult to wash afterwards and wondered how on earth the men got clean at home; it must have taken a lot of lading cans full to the very brim. Aunt Lizzie never gave the coalmen any tea.

In an old-fashioned wooden chair at one side of the range my uncle would sit smoking his pipe, very contented until my aunt saw him. 'Some folks leave muck for other folk to clean up!' She would fix him with a firm eye until he took the pipe out of his mouth and looked for somewhere to knock out the ash. 'And be careful. Don't get it on my hearth!' She would make remarks until he got up from the chair and went out, then explain that she could not abide him under her feet all the time. Quite cheerful once he was out of the way, she would let me help wash the things she had finished with. I had to be careful with a bowl used for making bread because they were not manufactured anymore with the outside rough to touch and the inside smooth and shiny at just the right angle for kneading the dough. Aunt Lizzie kept a close eye on me so I was nervous about knocking it against the stone sink or dropping it on the flags. I would never have recovered from such a catastrophe.

Just off the kitchen was a walk-in larder I was allowed to tidy if Aunt Lizzie was in a good mood. I had to climb on a wooden buffet to reach the top shelves and wipe the oilcloth, moving the pots of jam and marmalade and bottles of fruit labelled in spidery writing. Whole hams hung on hooks and so did onions – you just took one from the strings as you needed it. Chickens with feathers still on waited to be plucked, one of my uncle's jobs. At home we had the little pantry and the safe, and one mesh cover to keep flies away from cold meat but no bowls of cream or curd for tarts with muslin covers edged with coloured beads. The larder was a really nice place, except for the dead chickens. I was never allowed in there for too long in case I knocked something over. Another thing there was a big orange-coloured bin with a lid folding into two parts and another almost as big for keeping white and brown flour for all the baking Aunt Lizzie had to do. I think my uncle and the others ate a lot; good trenchermen, she called them. I would have loved to get flour out of the bins with the special wooden scoops, but no, it might have spilled, and 'Waste not, want not' was one of Aunt Lizzie's beliefs.

If my uncle said, 'Tha'd better have a bite with us lass, after all thy labours,' I often told a fib and said I was needed at home because of having to sit at the table on a sofa even worse than ours with horsehair from a very strong horse I thought. Also you were not allowed to speak and you could not get down early even though your legs were cruelly scratched, having to wait until everyone had eaten the last crumb. It took something like a cream sponge to tempt me to stay. When I got home my mother would say, 'I hope you made yourself useful?' She said my aunt Lizzie needed help in that house, she was a good wife and mother but did not show her feelings easily, having had a hard life. I was very interested to know about this but she said some other time. My uncle must have known the details and put up with being grumbled at.

The cousins were nice when they came to our house to see my mother and they had to put up with jokes about getting married if people were there. Dick used to take a girl to the pictures on a Saturday but Harry had nobody, he was always working anyway. My mother said it was no use thinking I might be a bridesmaid for either of them, they would have to go a long way to get fed as well as at home and no wonder they weren't in any hurry.

I did learn Aunt Lizzie's hard life was about having to work on the farm as well as having children but could not see why that was so bad. I thought feeding animals would be enjoyable, particularly cows with their soft noses and the way they smelled of the sweet hay and stuff they ate. Everyone said it was a pity my uncle had to give up farming when he was born to it and loved animals, especially horses, but of course he was getting on and could not manage without Harry and Dick taking over, which they did not want to do. Dick said there wasn't enough brass in it for either of them. So it was a great wrench when everything was sold, even his favourite mare called Polly. He wanted to keep Polly but my aunt said better be done with it all and the creature might have eaten them out of house and home.

Once my uncle talked to me about the days when he and

his brothers were young and how they had to help with the work before and after going to school. I did wish they still had the farm so I could have done the same, even missing school at haytime or when the potatoes were ready. Their school sounded very strict – they had to fold their arms and listen all the time and then do writing or sums, no talking allowed, the master handy with a big stick. He would throw chalk as hard as he could at any boy who wasn't clever and shout 'Thou great fool!' or 'Thou born ass!' but luckily not at the brothers. When I was really young, if my friends and I played schools in the Rec and I was the teacher I imitated this but they said it was not fair and could not happen nowadays in any school. Some teachers still shouted, I said.

My uncle and his brothers wore trousers that went over the knee and long socks knitted by their mother. They had shirts whiter than the other boys – an old photograph showed this, and there right in the middle was the stern master with a back like a ramrod. My uncle said their jackets looked tight because growing lads always needed bigger ones and when he burst out of his it was passed on to Arthur and Arthur's to John and John's to Thomas, their Sunday clothes the same. He was lucky to be first. In the end they could not all stay on the farm and in any case did not want to, but helped if they were near enough or in their holidays.

'It wor the same then, not enough brass in it,' my uncle said, 'if brass were thy be-all and end-all.'

The land had been in their family for a long time. 'Tha knaws,' my uncle said to me, 'it 'ud suit thee to look it up, per'aps later on, ye'd find we go back a fair way.'

I made up my mind to go and look at the graves in our churchyard and in other places when I could, though they might be hard to read if they went back to Queen Elizabeth's day. I wondered if there would be girls or ladies with my name. All the boys' names – William, Richard, Harry and Thomas – had been used a lot and of course there was Aunt Lizzie; perhaps *a lot of Elizabeths after the Queen. It made me feel more sorry for my uncle having to give up the land and I decided to tell him so when I got the chance; that was when he was digging his garden. 'Hard work never killed nobody, Uncle!' I began, and he stopped and looked down at me, his eyes wrinkling up.*

'Ahm noan se sure the facts'll bear thee out on that, lass.' He lifted another shovelful of earth, turned it over to slice it with the spade, 'By the look of thee tha's after summat else, information I might nut be prepared te give.' The spade sliced again, then he stopped and fished in the pocket of his baggy old trousers to find one of his favourite sweets. 'Tha knaws full well who to ask if tha wants to knaw owt abaht owt,' he said, handing over the Minto...

Mary was clearly taken with the idea of family history, all the Williams and Richards and Harrys, the wives helping on the farm as well as cooking, baking and sewing and knitting things for their large families. And going back in time as far as Queen Elizabeth. Her mind was filled with the wonder of it and perhaps not for the first time thoughts became words.

As they waited for the bus one very wet day, feet in wellington boots, she asked, *'What about in olden days, how did they manage without wellies? Specially farmers...?'*

Friends used to Mary's ways had shrugged without bothering to answer; farm talk was not new to them but there was a snake in the grass, Meg willing to engage, making it clear she was sick of hearing about the olden days and a little farm going back to Queen Elizabeth...

'An' even if ye did, so does everyb'dy, that's Histry, no need for a swelled head!'

The bus came and all except Mary could forget ... little

farm ... Queen Elizabeth ... swelled head ... woven into the rhythms of the old bus, to torture...

She was crushed, the core of steel mislaid.

Chapter 15

On Saturdays in term time and always during school holidays Mary took on the household shopping: the journals gave no reason but it must be assumed the mother was less able to do it. Shops unheard of now are described and others with familiar names no longer play a part in village life. Walking up Main Street was a reminder: a change of window or adjustments to brick or stonework reveals that conversion to a house has taken place.

At the top of Grange Road a shop sold sweets and tobacco as well as the newspapers and magazines people wanted. I liked going in there because Mr Brown didn't make you wait while he served older people who came in after you. He delivered papers and magazines riding a bike with a basket in front to hold them all. He waved a hand when he saw you and smiled even when pushing it uphill. His first name was Alastair, though of course I didn't call him that.

Crossing Aireville Terrace you came to the fishmonger where a boy I knew called Soapy worked for his father. If he was swilling the flags I was pretty sure he would try to get some water over me so I always did a quick skip outside there. In winter the fish was laid out in a nice pattern but in summer the slab was left bare because of flies. Further along you came to the cobbler's. Mr Purdy was usually busy though some fathers mended their family's shoes at home. Most people did not want the bother of getting a last and nails and having to buy leather and cut out the shapes of soles and heels to nail on. It would be quite difficult to do ladies' shoes at home; Mr Purdy always made a neat job of the small heels and putting just a little piece at the toe rather than a full sole. His shop had an unusual smell apart from leather and boot polish, I think it was from heel-ball, stuff put on after a repair to make them the right colour or like new: it had to be warmed before being carefully applied and I think that made the smell.

Mr Purdy had given the village something to talk about. He and his wife had longed for a child and luckily had the chance to adopt a little girl. They were getting along nicely when lo and behold Mrs Purdy had twin babies of her own, which was quite unexpected. Most people thought they had acted too hastily getting the first child, since the shop was hardly a gold mine. To my delight, one day the twin babies were in their double pram at the counter with not much room left for customers. Mr Purdy said his wife had taken Dorrie, the little girl, to Otley market to do the shopping but the babies had been as good as gold, not even waking when he started up a machine. He looked pleased and happy, so he could not have been feeling the pinch as everybody said.

Almost next door to the cobbler's was the corner shop where we used to buy some things but not all as it did not give Divi like the Co-op. Such money was small but mounted week by week until there was a nice sum at the year end. This was not used for treats in our case but was always very welcome. The errand boy at the corner shop was from a family of Scottish people and when it was the village fete this boy wore a kilt and did a dance, skipping high and landing neatly in between crossed swords without cutting his feet. On one occasion I noticed the feet were not clean underneath, though I might have been mistaken or the field muddy. Everybody said the boy was clever not only at dancing, he went to night school and did a lot of studying at home.

Next came the greengrocer and their boy was a friend of the sword boy and also of the one who worked for the butcher across the road. All the mothers were pleased with these boys for delivering the shopping; it was so much better than having to carry heavily laden bags themselves. After work the boys rode their own bikes round the village, stopping to chat with different girls, so they were well liked.

Going to the butcher's was not the best errand for me but I had to make the best of it. I disliked seeing meat there rather than animals alive in the fields. Mr Johns the butcher was a large man, broad and strong with a red face, always joking as he sliced your Sunday joint off a great side of beef and took it to a block to trim and tie up. He could sharpen a knife in a flash, laughing if you jumped as it clashed against the steel implement. Sometimes when he served a customer he would make a serious face and say, 'None of your bloody foreign meat 'ere missus, eh?' not swearing but taking a dig at the Co-op round the corner where meat in the window dripped pools of red. Mr John's shop was well cleaned and he wore an apron over his clothes which he did not allow to get too stained before changing it. One of the boy's jobs was to sweep and scrub the floor then spread sawdust over it: this stuck to shoes so you had to remember to check before going into the house. The wooden blocks in the shop needed scrubbing hard and poor George's hands got very sore in winter: the sword boy's life seemed much easier in the corner shop.

In the grocery section of the Co-op I usually got served by the manager, who knew me because he played cricket in my cousin's team and I often went to watch. He liked to say my cousin would be out first ball at the next match and unfortunately this sometimes happened. In the shop great mounds of butter, lard and cheese were kept on a wide shelf behind the counters. It was clever the way the assistants could guess how much to scoop off or cut with a wire almost exactly the amount asked for: you could tell it pleased them to get the right weight, but instead of saying so they pretended not to notice as if it was all in a day's work.

The Co-op had no delivery boy. All shopping had to be carried and got heavier and heavier on the way home, the worst being flour, half a stone at a time measured out from a huge sack at the back of the shop. I was only sent for flour if my mother really needed it, as bought bread did not taste right. Once, when I was carrying flour and some other things, the handle of the bag broke off so my arms were just about breaking as I hugged it all the way down Grange Road.

If we needed vinegar or treacle the shops near home were better because I had to take a bottle or jar for them to fill, and it was no use carrying those further than you had to. Vinegar poured so swiftly from the barrel that some would spill, but treacle oozed out slowly with plenty of time to close the tap before it dripped onto the floor.

One day, going to Aunt Lizzie's, I found a shop with marshmallow sweets I liked so much I went back every Saturday to buy them with my pocket money. However, the shopkeeper's wife discovered the sweets were fourpence an ounce not fourpence for a quarter of a pound as he thought. She sounded grumpy explaining this while Mr Dix stood by looking uncomfortable. The marshmallows weighed so light I got a whole lot for one penny before my luck ran out. After that I did not like going into the shop, with Mrs Dix keeping an eye on me in case I got another bargain. It would have been nicer there without so many things on the floor, empty boxes and sacks everywhere and things waiting to be put on the shelves. A sort of smell came from a back room which also seemed to need a good clear out. My mother often said I was good at tidying up but I knew I was the last person Mrs Dix would have asked to help.

Mrs Hardisty's shop was much nearer our house and I liked it there and if Mrs Hardisty's sister came to serve you it was like meeting an old friend as she had been my teacher before Mr Harris. I regretted having to leave both of them to go to the new school. The shop sold sweets and tobacco and also bread, cakes and buns with icing or cream but we never bought them – my mother baked all ours, which was cheaper though it made rather a lot of washing up.

There had been a shop on Main Street selling only cakes brimming with cream. We had those once for a special treat and they were delicious beyond words. The girl in this shop was quite young and rather fat. Her father already had another shop and opened this one especially for her. However, after some time the girl whose name was Nancy got much thinner and because her face was very pretty and she had nice fair hair she was soon snapped up by a young man who earned enough money without the cakes. People said Nancy got thin by using a roller but I do not know how. She made a lovely bride and church bells rang out for all the village to hear. Nancy's father paid for everything and I guess the wedding cake would have been of good quality and very special.

The shop was changed to sell wireless sets and they charged up the accumulators if people left them there for a while. I never bothered to look in the window as I did in Nancy's time. There was a furniture shop and a smithy where horses were shod and several public houses: we did not use any of them.

Chapter 16

The village shops have seen changes. There is no risk from sawdust at the butcher's and shoes are unlikely to have felt the touch of heel-ball. No marble scales demonstrate skill – packets are selected from a shelf.

Mary had taken on the responsibility of the shopping, watched the pennies like an adult and obviously been a great help to her mother, but her revelations had to be put aside because for all the talk and all the prettyfying of the house there was no bidder, no sale; the so-called holiday had accomplished nothing. At home an important date was looming, the annual test of the herd for brucellosis and tuberculosis. Always they got extra help for this but she played a main part. John would say he could manage but clearly she was needed and must go back. She raked the ash from the grate and tidied the hearth and put things ready for the morning.

It was a stroke of luck to find a place to park on the Grove near to the agent's offices in Ilkley. The firm had windows full of desirable properties for sale, no doubt some were 'deceptively spacious', especially those in the 'conversation area' described in the first version of the brochure for Number 6. Her man was chatting to a woman at the back of the room. He came forward bringing the familiar scent, but his smile lost brilliancy as he saw, unfamiliar in winter coat and hat, the owner of a property which had not proved at all desirable. An apology for not being in touch, the market slow, the time of year not quite right. It did not matter because she had come to say that operations must be suspended for a while, nobody sent to view unless for the second time and likely to make an offer. She gave a date after which he could telephone her in Scotland or get in touch with her neighbour. There was relief in the air as she left.

'I think you might say he was happy to see me off the premises,' she told Sandra afterwards.

She telephoned John and though he did say he could manage the test, relief was there too. She could imagine an almighty clean-up would follow the good news, the washing machine in action if he could remember how it worked. None of it mattered as long as the farm work got done, and that was beyond doubt – he would work long hours to keep everything up to snuff. Already she felt invigorated; it would be wonderful to be home doing the things she loved, the feeds, walking round the cattle, the last trip to the steading checking all was well. She could hardly wait to see the herd, and, of course, John. And the bulls – he would not have time to groom the Murray Grey, sort out the tangles in his curls; a treat to come. Meantime what could be done? Looking at the 'feature', inspiration came – she would bake a cake, John's favourite fruit cake to take back as a surprise and change from 'shop-bought' stuff: what she left would not have lasted the course. Like the cousins, John was a trencherman.

Even when a fire was lighted she had not tested the oven, using it only to warm ready-made meals from the supermarket. The gas rings sufficed for anything else and now and again she had eaten out. She would build up the fire and somehow test the oven temperature. There was also the small matter of a recipe, something to refer to if she could not remember the one used at home.

For once she had a list of things to shop for. Usually she went to the village and accepted what was on offer; with only herself to please it was not worth spending time on it. At home things were bought in bulk for house and farm as if a siege from some invading horde was on the cards. In any winter, Scottish weather could be that enemy hemming them in, the farm road blocked and deep in snow long after main roads were clear. Those careful supplies disappeared at a rate of knots, feed vanishing down throats made hungry by the cold and the demands of calves to be born in springtime when the world was kinder.

She caught the bus to Leeds. Looking at people waiting at the stop, she wondered if anyone had known her aunt or even her young self in days gone by, but no face was familiar. The journey was more interesting than by car, with time to look, remember, see what was new. It was difficult to realise the scope of change: beyond Bramhope cows were grazing but the green spaces became smaller. More of everything else, houses, shops, parked cars, signs, a good many of those. Increased traffic slowed to a crawl by road works; a few drivers tapped at the wheel with their fingers, but most seemed patient. There were Edwardian and Victorian buildings to be admired in the town and in one of the arcades an automated clock belled the hours and the quarters, figures from Sir Walter Scott's *Ivanhoe* striking mellow-toned bells with their fists. Arriving as the last chimes rang out, she exchanged smiles with others who stopped: for more than a century Robin Hood, Friar Tuck, Richard Coeur de Lion and company had given this pleasure. Sure of the exact time, she went to the market to buy the fruit for John's cake: luscious Greek raisins, sultanas, currants, and lemon and orange candied peel, whole not ready cut, a little green angelica, dark cherries and almonds. Eggs and butter she would get locally. Parchment paper to line the tin. Nutmeg? Mixed spice? She thought there was some in the cupboard but bought more just in case. This was going to be a cake!

Sandra came in as she prepared the tin, greasing it ready for double layers of parchment. All ingredients except the fruit were on the kitchen table. Now was the time to get confirmation of the recipe.

'I've done the fruit but...'

Sandra was laughing, 'Ye mean all that rigmarole with the colander and the tap running till the water's clear?'

'Well, yes, to make the fruit plump and juicy.'

'My God, I never would 'ave patience!'

'Have you a recipe you like then, not fussing?'

'Me? Well ... Marks and Spencers, Betty's if I'm flush which i'nt all that often.' She laughed, 'Your aunt tried te get me going, wanted to give me 'er book, but I said it'ud be a waste, I watched many a time though before she got frail ... that book should be somewhere.'

Together they found it, a small book with a thick cover, the recipes in a different hand, bold, not Aunt Mary's.

'Sandra! This cake recipe, it's the same as mine! The very same one! It must be...'

'Handed down! An' patience to do it, fiddle with all that...' She waved a hand, 'Handed down an' all!'

'In the genes!'

They laughed and then fell silent as the orange and lemon peel was chopped into tiny pieces to mix with the angelica, the almonds, the cherries and the plumped-up fruit, and the shade of Aunt Mary was there savouring the scents of it.

Sandra did not wait to see the final process, the generous measure of brandy stirred in before putting it into the prepared tin, the centre hollowed a little to produce the correct shape. With cartridge paper around the tin for extra protection, the cake at last in the oven, a weary eye saw the things to be washed up stacked high on the narrow draining board and overflowing into the sink. Conscience dictated this should be tackled before she relaxed. The bottle of Martell was still on the table so she poured a good measure into a glass to help her do the right thing.

Chapter 17

It was easier and quicker to go by train but luggage was limited to what she could carry. Wrapped in foil, the cake took up room in the suitcase but it had turned out well, golden brown with not a trace of burning as she had feared using an untried oven: she had accepted praise from Sandra and hoped for more at home. Sleek and modern, the train gave a better ride than the local one to Leeds; with luck, in a few hours she would be in Aberdeen.

When looking out of the window, reading the newspaper and attempting the crossword began to pall she had something in reserve, another offering from Aunt Mary. Returning the book telling of the shopping expeditions to the olivewood box, she had come across loose sheets of thin paper clipped together with a note which read, 'I had written this hoping Dennis might get it somewhere near his birthday and he would remember, and be amused. But it was too late...'

The letter was headed 'Birthday Boy'.

Some new houses were built on the way down to the Dam Stones and one of my friends moved there. Sometimes when you went down Mill Road you had to pass all the mill girls going home for their dinners. I was pleased if they waved or called out to me: they took up all the road linking arms and laughing and even singing sometimes. I never saw them at the end of the day, I expect they were too tired to sing then. Joan's mother thought the mill girls were a fast lot but I said they had to be – with those looms crashing and banging, it was the only way to avoid accidents, and she started laughing. I was not sure about her.

Their house was very nice with the same sort of new smell as Amy's, the same doors with no panels to dust and carpet right up to each wall, not just the middle of the room. The furniture was mostly new because Mrs Wilkinson thought their old stuff didn't look right. Most people said that was all very well if you had the brass but would rather do without than get it on the never-never, putting a little money down and then paying something each week until the debt was cleared. We didn't approve of that so our furniture was not much to look at.

Joan was one year and a quarter older than me and really nice though she told me a rude word: everybody knew it, she said, but I had better not mention who told me. I wished she never had, knowing it might slip out because I was not used to hiding any words at all, my trouble was talking when I should have the sense to shut up. Sometimes we went down by the river and over the stepping stones if the water was low enough. This was only during summer holidays and now mine were nearly over, the new school coming into my thoughts. When I told Joan I was nervous, she said, 'You're allus bothered about summat – if it weren't that it'ud be summat else!' We were at the mill goit where willows dipped into water that looked deep and still until after a while the surface rippled and a fish snatched at a fly; the sky had clouded over, making things darker. I thought it a very mournful sight, expecting Joan to agree, but she said, 'For Heaven's sake!' So I decided to go home.

It cheered me up that my tea was ready, and better still there was news of a birthday party and I was invited. It was a picnic at a secret destination; I guessed this might be through the railway tunnel beyond Peaseborough – it was a favourite place because the beck was nice and wide for jumping. Luckily the weather kept fine and I set off shortly after our dinner to meet the others at the house where Dennis was staying – he really

85

lived in Leeds. I was wearing stockings from my new uniform, long black ones which felt good. I had a giant bar of Cadbury's milk chocolate for a present but my mother said Dennis had better leave it behind as all the little gannets would make it disappear like snow in summer. When my mother made jokes the sides of her eyes went into little wrinkles which she said were crows' feet like their tracks in the snow, but her face was so nice nobody minded.

We had to carry our food in brown paper carrier bags, exactly the same in each one, so there was no need to squabble and Dennis had a cake already sliced to make it easy for him. It didn't take long to reach the secret place, which was exactly where I thought, and all six of us decided to eat first, so we set about the carrier bags in a hollow place sheltered from the wind. In fact it was seven of us or six and a half, because Leonard was forced to bring his sister Lucy who was not very old.

'Me mam sez if tha dun't want 'er I can't cum nawther — she 'as te go aht sumweear.'

Dennis had looked at him and at Lucy's little currant-bun face, then in a funny gruff voice said, 'Okay! Cum'on then!'

After a time we seemed to feel full without even a thought of the cake and decided to start building a dam. Dennis knew how to go about it and told us all except Lucy what to do. He wanted stones large and small, any bits of wood we could find and sods ... not swearing, only lumps of grass from the edge of the beck; he had a trowel packed in with his food. He made us take our shoes off and in my case my stockings, saying it would prevent getting into trouble for being wet, so I put them carefully into my empty carrier.

It was a really beautiful dam, piled high, hardly any water trickling away and above it a smooth and shining lake.

'Bloody good, that!' Dennis said. He stood in the water, his clothes streaked with mud and his freckly face as red as a beetroot: 'It'll mek a bloody good jump.'

86

But Reg and Ronnie didn't want to, maybe tired of 'Fetch us more wood! ... Stones, big 'uns! ... More sods!' All the hardest things.

'If tha'll gie us a bit o' cake Dennis, we'll jus' wish thee 'appy Birthday an' get off 'ome.'

The lake was a bit wide to jump. My feet just reached the edge and nearly slipped back the first time. We had several goes and Lucy watched. She seemed happy enough with the odd word from Lenny, we didn't bother much. Most of the afternoon she just sat trying to make daisy chains, sometimes talking to a little girl called Marigold who wasn't there. She was quite a sweet little girl, almost bursting out of her dress – 'as plump as a partridge' my uncle would say.

We were tiring and ready to agree when Dennis said, 'We'd better bust it afore we go...' We waded into the lake and began shouting, 'Bust the dam! Bust the dam! Bust it!' at the top of our voices. This got Lucy interested and she waddled close to the edge. Dennis told her to get back but she took no notice. When she slipped into the water the noise was enough to waken the dead, and our shouts faded to nothing. Lenny leapt to pull her out but she wouldn't budge, just sat howling, getting wetter and wetter.

We looked at each other. 'My God!' said Dennis like a grown-up. 'She rooars wors'n a bull cawf!' Once on dry land she shivered in between roars, making more row when I stripped the dress off and ordered Lenny to give her his jersey; winter and summer, he wore one to always be warm. He didn't want to and Lucy yelled and shivered, but Derek helped by saying, 'Go on daft 'ead, she'll dee o'cowd if tha dun't!'

Quickly I got my pumps on and put the dress into my carrier after squeezing as hard as I could to get the water out. Dennis put my stockings in his bag so they kept dry and I hurried Lucy off; they gave a last push to bust the dam and followed. Lucy had slowed a bit but began at full blast when nearly home, so no wonder her mother was at their gate. Unfortunately as I handed it over, the carrier also busted: it looked as if the colours in the dress had run together.

'Git inside, you!' she shoved Lenny. 'An' just ... you ... wait till your father gets home!'

We trooped back down the path and sat on a wall a bit further down. Derek brightened up. 'We never 'ad t'cake!' he reminded Dennis. Dennis felt in the bag and came out with my stockings. He tied one round his head like Davy Crockett and gave the other to Derek, who did the same. It made us laugh. We then ate our cake and it was so lovely we looked longingly at the piece left. 'Nay, fair do's!' Dennis decided after a moment. 'Ah'll jus' tek it for Len ... an' 'er!' Lenny was not available so he handed in the parcel and came back.

'She's still rooarin'!' he said, and we went home.

Chapter 18

It was wonderful to be home. Nothing mattered except that. She would get the house back to some sort of order, tackle floors, windows, loads of washing, dust everywhere though kitchen and bathroom showed signs of an onslaught. A pity she had given notice of returning, John had enough to do without 'umman's wark' as they called it in the Howe. Light-hearted and full of energy, she could not wait to get started.

The next morning was different, dark and confusing: it took time to realise where she was and why an alarm shattered the air in what seemed to be the middle of the night. Her mouth was dry from wine they had with supper; she was reluctant to get up and dress, wanted to think, remember their late visit to the steading and the animals asleep or cudding, so peaceful...

'You needn't come,' John's voice somewhere near, 'I can manage.'

Clothes from yesterday on a chair in a bedroom that was a tip, but all in good time, real work first.

'No! I want to, I'll find some things to wear...' Hair tucked into a cap, old jacket over old clothes, she pulled on newish wellies and went to get on with it.

Air crisp and cold: familiar sights and smells beginning where light from the steading breached the dark.

John had worked quickly, adding small bales of hay to what remained of large bales from the previous day. The cows were settled, all the jostling for position over and done: soft chewing sounds met the ear like the murmur of prayer. Giving out concentrates, specially made feedstuff to ensure a correctly balanced diet including vitamins and minerals came next, and this had its perils. The farm steading was unsuited to modern ways: a deep court when emptied of muck left the feeding troughs impossible to reach; cows could feed from them only if muck was left untouched day on day, week after week. The result would be a squelching morass with animals belly-deep in sharn and it was not on, hence the purchase of ring feeders and additional wall racks for young stock from the blacksmith at Monymusk. With plentiful use of straw bedding, the cows were dry and comfortable. To feed concentrates, so easy in a modern building where the farmer could by hand or by machine empty a sack evenly from one end of a long trough to the other without interference from the coos was far from easy with the ring feeding system. Carrying heavy sacks into the court to unload into rings surrounded by cows desperate to get at something so utterly delectable to them was risky. With both working like dervishes to beat the rush, it was bearable. With one person it could be a nightmare: once she had been overwhelmed, carried off her feet, had to press on the wide red backs of the enthusiasts to lift herself up and stop the pressure on her ribcage. Not funny at all.

However, now she was back they funnelled the stuff into the rings at a rate of knots and the coos settled quickly. After that effort they went to the narrow passage above the court to lean on the rails and look down: sweaty, breathing hard and laughing, they were a team again and they did what farmers love to do, they looked at their beasts.

'I stand and look at them, long and long...' said the poet in a far-off time, and he saw into a stockman's heart.

The young stock fed, time spent with the bull and

putting out supplies for the next feed, and they could take a break. While she went back to the house, John fed the geese and the tame pheasant always near them. Last in line, they could relax over their own food, discuss things, make plans. It came to mind that in the village she would scarcely have been out of bed, doing very little until Sandra came in for a cup of coffee and a gossip. John was aware of the change.

'What about yon lassie down there, could she cope with this?'

'If she had to! Trews instead of the miniskirt and smaller earrings, I reckon she would.' Another thought, 'And sort the house, go through it "like a dose of salts!" as my aunt said.'

'A kitchie-deem in a miniskirt! Every ferm should have one, er ... except when he's got the perfect wife!'

'Saved by the bell!' said the perfect one.

The pleasure at being back did not fade even as the day of the test grew closer. The 'holiday' had heightened her sense of how lucky they were to live in such surroundings. The work was hard and didn't stop at five o'clock, in fact didn't stop at all during calving or any of the crisis moments. And always the views took the breath away, of distant hills, their colours changing with the seasons until a covering of snow dazzled the eye. On the farm they had woodland, more trees bordering the river, and birds ... and rabbits, John reminded her by taking his gun.

'I'm going for half an hour or so, they're on the increase...'

The breeding habits of little bunnies made them undesirable and their warrens were a risk for cattle when their tunnelling neared the surface. All other things were cherished though, the wild birds, curlews, pheasants, ducks, seabirds galore, the farm a haven generally. Once they had a heronry but no longer; a nearby gamekeeper was suspected but they had no proof. The herons had been lovely to watch especially when they had young, the racket they made had been part of the farm and they were missed.

The days passed with the normal pattern of work, regular patrolling to check the stock, the slog of the feeds, a bit of housework and plenty of cooking. More of a hotpot man than a salad eater, John had quickly used up supplies left in the freezer. Re-fuelling, as he called it, had been difficult from local supplies but now hotpots and roast dinners restored him. By the look of the Aga he had done a fair lot of frying; it was hard to banish the frying pan but she would set limits. Not that he ever got chubby – annoyingly, he seemed to have hollow bones.

Test day came. Prepared up to the hilt as always, yet the unexpected could happen. Sometimes a vet was called to an emergency and was not on time so cows locked in the court ready for the 'blood-letting' became restless and inclined to panic. Bribing with extra hay worked for a while but not for long. However, delay was unavoidable and taken without resentment because another time it might be your emergency, your spot of trouble. The fact that testing was vital to ensure herds were kept free from infection did not make a test less of an ordeal. Stramash, meaning uproar, confusion, was a Scottish word that fitted. Usually they got the right result – an all-clear because the herd did not come in contact with other cattle and the farm had no immediate neighbours with grazing animals. Forestry land and the river Don were effective barriers.

Gavin and Gilbert arrived on time, joking and relaxed, in contrast to the nervous strain she tried to hide from them. John looked confident but she guessed he would be as glad as she would be to see the last poor beast go through the crush. Unaware of their captive state, the cows were still relishing the extra hay bribing them. When their nemesis arrived to take blood samples a number would be released into a gated-off area in front of the steading. From this area half a dozen would then be syphoned into the small adjoining space which narrowed, culminating in a railed passage leading to a cattle crush and the waiting syringe. It was her job to keep animals from backing out from that passage by placing an iron bar behind each one – a mucky, sweaty job, but she was used to it and at the same time she could alert the vet to the name of each cow: he was supplied with a list of names and official numbers so the samples could be identified.

John would be at the crush to entrap the head and hold it at an angle, enabling the vet to take the blood sample; then, head released and gate opened, the animal entered a final gated area. The procedure was rarely as simple as planned, as cows can be temperamental, frisky and nervous, liable to panic, with the odd one becoming belligerent. That was why after each annual session, the farm diary had tales of mishap, frustration, damage, even injury, but always recorded, 'We are exhausted!' sometimes with an expletive.

However, 'Maun dee's a gweed maister' and the test began.

All in all things went well. David, their vet, was efficient, deft with the syringe and willing to give a hand with anything that speeded the process. Gavin worked without fuss, used to the part he played, and no words could describe Gilbert as a cattleman – he was simply 'the tops'. John's eyes took in everything, foreseeing trouble, and calm at dealing with it. Eventually, to the relief of all, the last cow went through the crush, the bull in his pen behaving like a gent. All samples packed away, the test was over.

To the kitchen for food and a glass or two of the water of life, the moment savoured, perhaps most of all by cows free for a little while from the hand of man.

Chapter 19

The aftermath of a test was always the same – extra work had to be fitted into the day's routines to return things to normal: it meant shifting heavy gates, moving things back into place and giving the young stock their share of the pens in front of the steading. At that time and for days afterwards, whatever happened in the way of large or small mishap, dealing with it bore no comparison to the upheaval when the whole suckler herd was involved. Before a test Baden-Powell himself could have found no fault; preparation was intensive, they foresaw the worst that could happen, and were mightily relieved if it did not. But all the effort was worthwhile. When clearing up was completed by flushing away sharn, the power-washer leaving everything glistening from its onslaught, it was also a shriving of souls, anxieties drained, the spirit left bare. Bringing the mail during the stramash of the test Postie stopped to say, 'Hard wirk's nae easy!' and someone answered as expected, 'Wirkin' hard's nae better!' which was true, but like the man who wore tight shoes and enjoyed taking them off, there was pleasure in watching the vet ease his G-Wagen doon the road with the little phials tucked safely away, and euphoria lasted for a while.

Christmas came and went, and as always in Scotland, with much more effect came the New Year's spate of visits and general bonhomie and the giving and taking of drams of the special stuff. Later in January heavy snowfall made life difficult. Coos content to stay in the court, with appetites increasing as temperatures fell gave a reminder that stocks of hay and straw had to last until springtime. Traffic stopped on the minor roads, and the farm road lost shape and merged into the whiteness of the parks beside it. Often winter brought isolation, a pocket of time when they were suspended from all but the daily work. In a silence tempered only by little noise from the courts or the drone of a high plane, anything voiced was given edge, the timbre changed. Once, taking a breather after the last feed, she looked over the wide Howe to where the sun was beginning to close the day. She smiled, remembering her aunt as a child.

'I will lift up mine eyes...' she said aloud.

Experience made John add, 'Watching where I put my feet!' but he left what he was about and came to witness the white world turn gold, redden, soften to a glowing rose deepening over the braes until it too gave way to shadow and reminded them to switch on the lights.

The red Land Rover brought Postie with a letter in estate agents' language telling them there was an offer on the village house, not an offer at the asking price, or one near that sum, but nevertheless an offer which 'might warrant the most careful consideration in view of...' Boiled down, it questioned whether it was worthwhile hanging on to a house nobody else seemed to want and why not take the money? It was the quiz show *Deal or No Deal* the contestant a fair distance from the quizmaster and not quite free from imprisonment by weather. Without a name for the prospective purchaser, it was hard to decide: was it someone worthy but unable to rake up the required sum or, horrible thought, a kind of rip-off by a 'buy to let' person with a nice taste in motor cars, knowing the ropes?

'It might be worth going to find out.'

'Another "holiday", leaving you with all the work?'

'My back is broad...'

Eventually she accepted the idea because, as John pointed out, it was England not Timbuktu, she could be there and back in no time and she might regret taking what seemed the easy way out. Besides that, she had a car down there which had to come back sometime.

It was a relief to find he thought as she did that selling cheap to save effort seemed like betrayal, demeaning a generous gift because it was inconveniently situated.

Her arrival brought Sandra, full of jokes and gossip, the children smiling, Darren carrying her bag. Aunt Mary and the child Mary almost out of mind in the busy life of the farm, returned as she sat with a welcome cup of tea, enfolded by the warmth and charm of the little house. It was almost a homecoming. After telephoning John she needed words with the agent but decided to wait until the next day. With a clearer mind, she could listen to his facts, allow for a natural pressure to achieve a sale and take time to think. Early to bed, she lay wondering how John's day had gone and, picturing the last visit to the steading, fell asleep.

Up betimes, she telephoned to Ilkley to make the appointment. At 2.30 in the afternoon it was later than she wanted, but it was nice to return to the routine of coffee with Sandra. Surprised to hear that some of the first people to view had been back again, she vaguely remembered having written off two of them as unlikely purchasers. Sandra of course did not know whether any had made an offer.

'I have to get back in a few days, Sandra.' They sat

over the coffee cups, conscious that their friendship, pleasant though it was, might be brief.

'You have to pick the right sort for my sake!' A smile brightened into mischief. 'Six foot … a bit rich an' sexy with it!'

'And no wife to spoil your fun!' It was sealed with the last drop of brandy from the cupboard.

The Grove in Ilkley was, as ever, busy with drivers competing for parking spaces, young women with prams and dogs on leads, older couples, the men interested in Betty's fine display of food, their companions in front of clothes shops or looking at shoes, well-dressed, leisurely people. She walked to the office to hear more about the offer for Number 6.

The agent was not at a desk and for a moment she thought there was a mix-up, but then a girl came to usher her into an office and there he was behind a desk spread with papers. He rose to offer his hand, hoped she was well, and, slightly bashfully but with evident pleasure, answered the unspoken question.

'Er, as you see, I've been promoted, I'm the manager now!'

She had to be glad for him, for the nice suit, the generous shirt cuffs, a tie not in the least flamboyant, the slightly plumper face implying that here was a man who lunched. It seemed their exchange would be less hurried than formerly. While he turned the pages of a file, reading them carefully, she looked around at pleasant watercolours, the substantial desk, comfortable chairs and what looked like a drinks cupboard; in addition there was computer apparatus and the shining wooden floor common to modern office life. The room lent itself to considered opinions, civilised interchange, but any pressure could be subtle and difficult to withstand.

He looked up from the papers. 'The previous manager

wrote to you about an offer received, which I would not advise you to accept – that is, unless, well, you want a quick return. If you are prepared to wait a bit longer I think we can approach the asking price.'

It was unexpected. She had come inclined for battle because it mattered to her who got the house, the necessary good neighbour with or without the desired qualities.

'Could I ask who made the offer?'

'Better not, unless you are going to take it!'

They were getting on terms, improvement coming with status; behind the driven salesman was this responsible young man she found more likeable. They discussed what was to be done and she agreed to fund more advertisements in a month or so. Later she wondered if he had twisted her arm about the new expense but did not begrudge it: for the time being Aunt Mary's house was safe. It also crossed her mind that the drinks cupboard remained locked.

Chapter 20

It was nice to settle on the Arthur Darbyson sofa, the fire giving out a good heat, the olivewood box beside her offering things in her aunt's life she might have heard about but taken up with her own concerns, had not troubled to remember. Dennis, presumably the focus of the writing, was there only as a child: adult Dennis remained a shadowy figure, the name on the church wall with all the other names, someone not talked about. She remembered silences, and being told not to ask questions.

There were more loose pages and another note reading: 'Too late to send' and 'He knew Mrs Firth'.

I had a cup of tea with Mrs Firth at No. 11 and she was upset because the vicar and his wife called when she was 'all in her muck' as she put it. It proved a warning not to be too house-proud, remind me if ever our little house takes me over. By the way, blackleading is your job, hall-marked. Did you know about the envelopes for the church collection? Mr P-P and his wife deliver them personally, maybe hoping to get more people involved but most folk are hard pressed. However, the visits did keep us in touch, Aunt Lizzie tolerated them and gave them a fine tea into the bargain but even there the dogs were a problem, I remember a cat upstairs in a sulk until they had gone. Mrs Firth was clear about the 'blasted sausage dogs with their little legs' and about 'people like that who never did a hand-stir themselves...' It is well-known that Mrs Firth is house-proud, spends a deal of time scrubbing floors and cleaning and polishing though she has no children to mess things up;

it is just her way. Pristine paintwork, a brass door-knocker shined each day, the perfect white of sheets on her washing line drew admiration but in the heart people felt that life was too short and anyway you all eat a peck o' dust afore you dee, so they settled to read Woman's Own *before it was time for the children to come home from school wanting their tea.*

Mrs Firth must have been first on the vicar's list and when the knocker rattled she was in the middle of cleaning the kitchen range. 'There was I in a mucky apron, doing the blackleading!' She had to ask them inside, into the living room with chairs up-ended on the table and rugs rolled up, plants and ornaments removed. Mrs Palmer-Paterson, undaunted had lifted chairs for herself and the vicar and settled to business, the little dogs muddling their leads around her legs. The vicar, said to know Latin and Greek and be very brainy, leaves parish matters to his wife who has a practical turn of mind. Mrs Palmer-Paterson's voice is musical, bears the imprint of a good school and is pleasant to listen to. Intent on getting help with a Bring and Buy sale, she gave details of time and place and names already signed up to man the stalls, then said she badly needed someone like Mrs Firth to take charge. The vicar nodded and Mrs Firth listened but later explained, 'I just couldn't take in what she said with the house all upside down and smelling of blacklead and so cold ...' It was a rotten day, raining, so there were foot and paw prints to worry about but worse was to follow, beyond endurance for her. The vicar himself is not immune to the mesmeric quality of his wife's voice, so neither of them and certainly not Mrs Firth noticed the little dogs not merely straining at the leads but desperate to be outside, one driven to lift a leg on a rolled-up rug, mistaken for a fallen tree if you were charitable.

As yet Mrs Firth cannot manage that or forgive the trespass, but did laugh when I told her one of the dogs had produced a puppy and I saw the vicar cradle it in his arms as if about to christen it. I dared to point out the folly of so much blackleading and suggested having the range taken out. Time will tell!

I heard about another house-proud lady: Jack at work said years ago he and his wife went to a boarding house in Bridlington for a week and the landlady was something of martinet, ruling everyone with a rod of iron, including her German husband, a kindly man who tried to smooth things over. From the start they felt she did not want people in her house spoiling the perfection of it and their little daughter got it wrong on the very first day by having sand in her shoes. The landlady, Mrs Saunders, had snatched at the little girl's hand, taken her to the front door and quite forcibly explained that next time she must empty her shoes before coming inside. You can imagine the effect on a small child unused to any but the gentle ways of Jack and his wife. A screwed-up mouth, gimlet eyes and a sharp voice had been enough to start panic, and for days shoe-shaking and a frantic search for betraying sand meant returning to the house for meals became a nightmare. Hers were not the only shoes waved about and shaken – the edict was observed by all, though mutterings could be heard in the dining room. Mr Saunders tried to help by keeping a dustpan and brush handy to scoop up offending grains.

In the town there was a baker's shop with wide windows and shelves overflowing with cakes and pastries and always in the afternoon people queued for something to take back for tea. Most people supplied their own food for the landlady to cook or serve – it was much cheaper than staying in hotels. On their last whole day Jack and his wife gave the choice to the little girl, thinking it would distract her from the anxiety which increased with every step closer to Beaulieu, aptly named only in terms of being very clean. Christine took the job of choosing seriously, examined every item and took time, too much time as it turned out, hesitating between small cakes with real cream and long buns with icing on top. She settled on iced, a housewife in embryo going for bulk. Insisting on carrying the bounty, she held it aloft like her offering at Harvest Festival, the proud, careful provider: it made them a little late.

They had not known that Mrs Saunders refused to serve tea in 'dribs and drabs' as she put it and that everyone was seated at the tables with the starched white cloths, cruet, plates, cups and saucers, the pats of butter and little jugs of milk, waiting, all waiting for Mr Saunders to bring the food and Mrs Saunders to mash the tea.

Even Jack quailed at the sight of Mrs Saunders as she snatched up the bag. A howl as Christine realised she had forgotten to shake for sand and looking at her feet they heard rather than saw the angry wasp zoom from the bag to settle on Mrs Saunders' cheek.

Jack told us with great relish how the dining room came alive, people smiled as they ate, and the talk...

'Poor owd lad! 'E 'ad te kill it, she med 'im!'

'It were doomed onnyroad...'

'Does ta mean fatally poisoned?'

'Nay, doomed fer it nivver wiped its feet afore it stung 'er!'

Only Christine truly regretted the wasp and ever since has been careful about buns with icing.

What a pity the beck-jumping and dam-busting and house-proud ladies were never posted for Dennis. Letters would be all-important. Recently there had been documentaries about the war on television, and in one men were shown getting mail and sharing news in the mess of a destroyer. Dennis might have been proud of Mary's letters and read out those pages to amuse his mates: but for him and for all of them everything had ended. The words 'too late' epitomised the tragedy of it.

Chapter 21

Another book of carefully written pages illustrated the closeness between neighbours who helped each other in a way that may have been lost now when people do not stay in one house for a lifetime. The Wrights were important for Mary and her mother, and there was mutual benefit.

When I was a very small weepy infant afraid of my own shadow Nelly Wright from next door but one certainly looked after me, took me under her wing and tolerated my obsession over a snake I saw in a tree, or did I imagine the horrible thing? I made her walk on the far side of the road and even then she had to drag me past that particular tree. We were friends for a long time. In fact we were close to all the family, though my mother did not like it if Mrs Wright gossiped in front of me or got too curious about our situation. Another neighbour used to say Mrs W was the eyes and ears of the village but most of what she said was harmless. My mother warned that little pigs have big ears so I learned very little except from Nelly. Her mum sent Dave, Mr Wright, if we needed help: he was quiet and rather gentle, getting on with things without fuss. Once they had a visit which had enormous impact and my mother helped by lending things for the occasion and a listening ear afterwards. The basis of it was money or the thought of it.

When Mrs Wright got the letter announcing a visit from an uncle who had a lot of 'brass' it turned her world upside down as if an archangel was in descent. It has to be said that housework was not a priority at No. 10. Easy-going Mrs Wright looked after the family in her own way, giving plenty of love and comfort. Her kitchen range never looked like the one in Mrs Firth's kitchen, but they fed well, with the frying pan used a lot and bread from a shop rather than the oven. You can imagine the prospect of Uncle Calvert staying the night as well as for most of a whole day. My mother turned up trumps with two vases Mrs Wright admired; she planned to get flowers for them from Otley market. In addition, there was a white damask table cloth and some pretty little knives with pearl handles we never used and a bedspread kept for the special occasions which were rare for us too. But first there had to be a grand clean-up followed by baking and plans for breakfast and an evening meal, should that prove necessary. No wonder there was panic. Nelly told me her mother thought she might benefit from Uncle Calvert's will, being the favourite one in the family. At his wife's funeral he said she was the very spit of the dear departed and looking at her reminded him of the loss and how the Lord moves in a mysterious manner. Nelly said he bowed his head as he said that and gave her mother a little pat, adding that she must keep in touch. Nelly made me swear not to repeat any of this or she would be skinned alive. Though nature cried out in protest, for a few days the house was in charge of a lesser Mrs Firth trying to put things to rights, and everyone was roped in – Dave, the boys, and Nelly, who told me she had begun to hate Uncle Calvert and prayed something would happen to stop him coming. Then it was time for the baking and here Mrs Wright began to worry. She knew about practice making perfect but had never practised baking the things she wanted to put on the table. Sponge cakes can be light as a summer breeze; a Dundee cake needs an even spread of fruit rather than in a layer at the bottom; pastry must be crisp and easy to digest. The scrubbed kitchen table, the bowls and whisks, spoons and measures, the grater and the piles of ingredients waited as Mrs Wright summoned courage and energy and, regretting her trips to the baker's, began to earn her legacy. It was late before she joined Dave in the small bedroom, their own made ready in case Uncle Calvert decided to stay, new sheets and the nice cover were on the bed, a Bible and an alarm clock near it.

The day came. I remember hanging about to catch a sight of the visitor, unsure what to expect. I saw Nelly and the others in their best clothes, popping out to look for the car. I knew from Nelly that the table was a wonderful sight, groaning with food beautifully set out on the damask cloth and flowers in a low bowl; with taller flowers from the market our vases were on the sideboard. Nelly said the boys had promised to behave and not argue as usual but wait patiently for the visitor to choose. They were going to say, 'For what we are about to receive' like at Christmas dinner. I did not see anything at the time and only from Nelly and later on from what Mrs Wright told my mother did I hear what the uncle was like and what happened when they sat down to eat.

Uncle Calvert was not short and fat and jolly as I imagined, but lean and miserable looking, quite the opposite, Nelly said. He did not come in a Rolls-Royce but in the old taxi from the station and they did not see him tip Irwin Clark. Mrs Wright was anxious for them to sit at table, knowing the boys would be hungry and might not be able to hold out. They said grace and waited for Uncle Calvert, who knitted his brows as each morsel was offered to him. 'It's a right good tea lass,' Dave said, smiling and proud, 'fit for a king!' But choice did not come easy and the brows were close together. Mrs Wright felt bewildered by Uncle Calvert's face, and the words coming from a quite unpleasantly pursed mouth.

'Ee Vinnie! Ee lass!' A shake of the head. 'As I tell't thee afore, tha's just like thy aunt Polly, the very spit! God rest 'er soul.' His eyes were on the wonderful spread. 'Not to speak ill of the dead, but she were prodigal ... food, clothes, owt there was. No care for the morrow!' He noticed the tall flowers and burst out again, 'T'same show, flowers an' all! ... An wheer does the brass cum from, I ask? Who's t'paymaster?' – a question *left hanging like the Sword of Damocles over the tired doppelgänger. In the stunned silence he had asked for a piece of cheese: 'I'll thank thee for a bit of Cheddar an' a small slice of loaf 'll do me nicely…' There was Gorgonzola, which cost a lot and was thrown away in the end because nobody could stand the smell, there were segments of cream cheese wrapped in silver paper, but not a shred of humble Cheddar in the house.*

He did not stay the night. Nelly said her mother slept badly and her dad took her breakfast up to bed but she was still in a sulk when she got up. The boys tucked into sponge cake for their breakfast. Later over a pot of tea Mrs Wright told them all she wasn't bothered who got the brass: behind her hand she told Dave that so far as she was concerned Uncle Calvert could go to aitch ee double ell.

There is an addendum written about the later time when much had changed for Mary and the Wrights. It is placed after the account of Uncle Calvert's visit, a postcript bringing the writing up to date. Perhaps office training prompted this, to close the file on Number 10 as it were. The house has new people, yet the association with Nelly lingers:

The new people in Nelly's old house are very different. Mr Kilner is one of a family owning several shops in the village and his wife is conscious of that. They have one child called Cleone of all things; I intend to look up the origin when I remember. Coupled with the surname it sounds well, as my old teacher might have said, it has euphony. She seems a nice little girl. The mother keeps a close eye on her, dislikes her playing out at the back with the children from Number 12 for instance and I wonder if that can last. An only child will find that little gang attractive, they are a bit cheeky but full of life. As Mrs K is quick to point out, Mr K is a director of the family business, so why such a modest house in our little row? Surely

Station Road or a detached house on Bradford Road would suit them better. Perhaps it is only a temporary stop. A number of people visit them, all rather nicely turned out. Mr K is tall and broad-shouldered and they make a handsome pair, obviously respectable which counts a lot, so I must sheathe my claws and look to find something beyond the flim-flam.

I can't help harking back to Nelly's family in that house. They were good neighbours. Nelly went to train as a nurse at St James Hospital and did very well, but when her father got a new job in Hull she moved there. We wrote for a while and then tailed off, as usually happens. I imagine she could be married now, she grew up bonny and judging by my experience would be perfect with a family. Their move came just after the funeral, so they were here for all of her time.

Chapter 22

Shortly after their neighbour's hopes of riches vanished Mary and her mother had a visitor the child was perceptive enough not to mention to her friend. To see Aunt Lizzie came one of the family who had gone to seek his fortune elsewhere, the one settling in Canada to farm and raise a family there. He was Will Pawson, a very much nicer man than Uncle Calvert, and Mary knew it.

When he walked up the path I thought it must be a mistake because we did not know anyone so big, like a giant he seemed to me at that time. His clothes were different – the jacket and trousers did not match and it looked as if he had put them on without noticing, but I learned they were not keen on suits in Canada and preferred this way of dressing called casual wear. I saw later one of his jackets hung loosely on his shoulders, another was smaller and he was bursting out, unable to fasten the buttons: it made me realise being so large was a problem. Uncle Will had left England when times were bad and had done well over the years. He was making the trip now to see the family and anyone who might remember him. He looked unforgettable to me.

We got used to seeing him at our fireside in our widest chair, which was not quite big enough. He would sit sometimes telling us about his farm or his wife and boys or he would just sit smoking his pipe and thinking, perhaps wondering if they were all right without him. I really loved his face and spent time trying to puzzle out why there was something so familiar about him. Afterwards I saw it was the picture in my bedroom, not the shepherd but the big old English sheepdog at his feet, the moustache of shaggy hair, the kind eyes and sweet, rather sad expression, a country dog at home only in the open air. That was true of Uncle Will; he loved walking, especially on the moors, with anyone who could spare the time. Dick said that at the Cow and Calf rocks he stood for a long time looking at the view of Ilkley. It was like a poem he learned once, about someone on a mountain looking far into the distance, but he could not remember exactly. He thought I was sure to come across it one day, and I did – I found this poem by Keats and think it was the one he meant:

> Then felt I like some watcher of the skies
> When a new planet swims into his ken,
> Or like stout Cortez when with eagle eyes
> he stared at the Pacific – and all his men
> looked at each other with a wild surmise –
> Silent, upon a peak in Darien.

Dear Uncle Will was certainly stout. He was eager to discover places he knew as a boy and was keeping a diary for his wife and family and friends in Vancouver Island. Harry and Dick went with him at weekends and whenever they had time off work. Talking to my mother about the trips they said at times he seemed disappointed, most likely confused by all the building that had gone on over fields he roamed as a boy, the meadows that were no longer there, but when they took him on the moors he brightened up and said it was grand to sniff the air again and everything was the same. I know what is so good about the moors: as you climb away from the road things change, and the loneliness is not fearful, you are so taken by the wind and the emptiness going on and on and being nearer the sky. Stony paths lead up beside grass the sheep crop short so your feet slip walking on it. Little becks find a way down past gorse in flower most of the time. In autumn you find bilberries to pick and the bracken turns colour and all of it gives out something for you to breathe that is pure and sweet and is only from moorland, not from anywhere else.

We missed Uncle Will when he went home to Vancouver Island and to this day I remember him clearly. One of his tales was so far out of my experience that it seemed to be from another world. When they were small two of his children had to walk several miles to school and the most direct way was along a railroad track which had very few trains each day, but they were used to the situation and in no risk of getting run over. I fancy I would have been looking over my shoulder for most of the way, pretty sure the train would take me by surprise. For company and for protection their dog went with them and that was to prove important, as one day, prowling along towards them came a cougar or mountain lion sometimes found in the lonely places of that country. When the cougar came closer, his ears flat against his head, he looked ready to spring and their dog sensed the danger. Bravely he stood in front of the children, snarling and baring his teeth, making little jumps towards the wild animal, warning him not to try anything. Naturally this made things worse, the cougar is a very fierce creature and he had made up his mind to get something to eat. The dog's hair was on end and he was going crazy, the snarls more frantic and getting hoarse as well. To help him the children began to shout and stamp their feet, waving their arms about, even swearing loudly and altogether putting on a fair show. After one or two feints and dodges the beast gave up and slunk off down the side of the track. Again I think I would have died of fright but the children picked up their schoolbags and went on, planning to tell their teacher and the other children why they were late. Of course Uncle Will was proud, especially of Flash the dog, and eventually the story got into the local papers. In time a London newspaper, the Daily Mirror, ran the tale and awarded Flash a gold medal. Uncle Will was invited to take him to London to be in a parade of dog heroes at Crufts but it was too far away and they did not think Flash would enjoy the trip.

Writing about visitors and also about Flash reminded me of calls made regularly by well-known village dogs called Bobby and Nip. Nobody was sure where they came from. They spent the days together going from house to house where they had friends ready to give them something to eat in case they had no real owner. If you asked, seeing them walk away from a house, you were told, 'Nay, we just give 'em a bite like most folks, like tha does thissen.' They may have been stray dogs but did not starve: Bobby was quite plump with a jolly look about him, Nip was thin like a greyhound but his coat was black and shiny and he ate as readily as his friend. We never minded them – well, perhaps Puss did, but she was too comfortable and lazy to bother. Bobby looked as if he was smiling and his tail was always on the wag. If you met them anywhere you felt you had to stop and say hello and tell them to take care and watch out for cars. Their visits were good for me when I was little. If I did not like anything it was no use saying there were starving children in Africa and I should eat everything on my plate, I knew who would eat it for me. Sometimes if it had been raining the two did smell a bit but we never turned them out.

Every year in the summertime Mrs Frazer came to see my mother. She was from London and you could tell she was different. My mother made friends with her when she came to visit a daughter who had to leave Mrs Frazer on her own for a lot of the time. Mrs Frazer's clothes were elegant, usually black and of good quality, but I remember her voice most of all, so clear and soft and of course she did not use Yorkshire words. My mother thought she must have been a great beauty once and you could see it still. During one of her visits Bobby turned up, alone this time and luckily not wet so we could still smell the perfume Mrs Frazer used. She said, 'What a sweet creature you are!' to Bobby and he settled at her feet. We chatted over a cup of tea and it was not until she got up to leave we realised what Bobby had been up to, hidden by the long black skirt she wore. A pretty thing around her neck, made entirely of feathers and reaching almost to the ground, was called a feather boa, and some of this long scarf was cradled between Bobby's paws; he was trying to bite and possibly eat it. We were dismayed but Mrs Frazer did not seem to notice, perhaps she did not want to make a fuss. I thought there was still plenty left as a fine scarf and after all it was summertime, so did not scold Bobby. My mother had to smile when I said it was the first time he had hunted a wild boa.

Chapter 23

She woke late, a weakish sun already at the window, but with no coos and calves and bulls to feed, no geese desperate to be out of the shed that kept them safe from the fox on the hill, she savoured being able to snuggle down and think about the little house and her reluctance to part with it. Reading about the two uncles she had lost count of time, absorbed in the memoir, the 'langsyne' of her aunt in the spik of the north-east. And now her own day was a blank page. What to do? ... Walk, where? ... Shop, what for? A luxury, having time ... a rarity broken by the telephone ringing and having to go downstairs to answer it.

Having heard she was at the house, the caller would be pleased if they could meet. Almost as an afterthought came the explanation that he had worked with her aunt for many years and his name was Roland Barr. The voice was diffident but there was no need, she remembered her aunt talking of people at her office and being on visiting terms with them and their families; it would be nice to meet him. It was settled that he would come at eleven-thirty for a cup of coffee. So much for the tabula rasa. She bathed and dressed quickly, glanced round the already tidy house and prepared the tray. If Roland required sugar she would have to borrow from Sandra. That pointed the need for shopping for a few things to tide her over the next few days.

Roland seemed mild like his voice. Tall, thin, clean-shaven, he wore the sort of suit her father used to wear, the everlasting type of thornproof tweed. The trousers were pressed, the shirt blending in nicely, nothing to startle the eye. Maybe not the style to be seen on market days in Otley, Roland had not succumbed to the comfort of trainers, his grey hair, cut 'short back and sides', was innocent of the baseball cap. She liked the look of him.

'Ah, this room, the stove...' A face softened with memories she could not share made it clear Roland had been fond of her aunt. Could this man have been more than a good friend? She could picture him supportive when the future lay in ruins... And it could have blossomed, her aunt encouraged to keep on writing as catharsis and because she had a gift... She had to stop, resist. The obviously respectable old boy not in the house five minutes before an adulterous liaison was suspected. John would have been quick to see imagination running riot.

Roland was remembering the house...

'She was comfortable here, this range better than the old one because it didn't need blackleading, she couldn't do with that. Homely it was, and is with the rug... She was sensible, didn't overdo the housework like the woman a few doors away, not there now, I suppose.'

He was nice, a gentle kind of man: somehow solitary as if there was no wife or anyone, no partner in the modern way, but soon he mentioned a daughter, a daughter with a family also living in Otley.

'She keeps me up to snuff!' said a little ruefully, 'and there is always one of them, her or Tom the husband or one of the boys telling me how out of date I am, wanting me to get a computer or a mobile telephone...'

They talked of the changes to Otley, the printing works, machine shops, the mills not only in Otley but in Burley, Addingham, Skipton, all gone; Sir Titus Salt legendary, but his great mill touted as a focus for tourists and modern art.

He stirred his coffee. 'At Dawson, Payne's you know, the machines went all over the world, I used to send chaps to service them. In those days if you were the one trusted with the job it meant getting a glimpse of other working lives, not just sunning yourself on the beach.'

'Did my aunt work with you on that?'

'At first, then over the years she became a sort of amanuensis, looked after the contracts, oversaw the catalogues, a bit of everything. They used to say the walls would fall down without her.'

He asked about the farm, said her aunt thought it a wonderful place, with the river and the woods and of course the animals. 'She said you worked hard, probably too hard...'

'That's true enough. There's no cut-off point when you clear a desk and get the bus home. The college people tell us to bear in mind the amount of time we spend, to cost things out and abandon schemes that are labour intensive; even animals qualify! But it isn't like that, you don't abandon Poppy because she's apt to get into a terrible mess and won't feed her calf, you spend hours on them...'

He smiled and nodded but could not know. She wished she had not brought Poppy into it, Poppy with her udder plastered in sharn, the calf miserable and not allowed near. It seemed wrong to be sitting over the coffee cups when John could be up to the eyes. There was certainly a gulf between her life and Roland's and only the fragile memory of her aunt bridged it.

As he got up to leave he asked her to lunch if she could spare the time: he was a fair cook, he promised. They agreed to meet on the following day, at twelve by the Jubilee clock and it was just a step from there to his house.

Sandra was interested to hear how the visit had gone. She had seen Roland before, and he had been at the funeral with one or two other people from the office.

116

'A nice chap. Good-looking even now. Never my type of course! I used to tease your aunt about what went on in offices, stuff in my Sunday paper. She said people like me came to a bad end and deserved to. She liked a laugh.'

The day had evoked memories of this different person, assured, liking to laugh, someone a long way from the child who quailed at the SHOUT of a teacher...

She had not mentioned the writing to Roland or queried why it continued after Dennis. Perhaps he was unaware it existed. The idea of liaison was fading because Roland did not fit...

The house in Otley was stone-built in a road once leading to a railway station; a charity shop and one or two others seemed out of place in the approach to the sober detached houses there.

I know it's too big for me, but it was in a very good part of the town when we first came, and of course we had family. Not far to walk to work either!'

'Like us, we walk down the garden path.'

Hall, stairs, rooms on either side, kitchen straight ahead, solid, practical, desirable for sure, she could visualise the brochure. They went into the kitchen.

'Do you mind? To be honest I don't use the dining room much except if they are all here, the family, and then my daughter takes over.'

'It's fine, and a good smell from there!' Like at home, the Aga made the kitchen a haven. 'We rely on ours, as you can imagine.'

Beef casserole, roasted potatoes, plenty of greenstuff, the usual sort of meal with a nice pudding. It was a change to have it cooked for her and a surprise that there was wine. Relaxed, they talked, first about his wife and a long illness; he had brought up the children, the older one living in Australia now and married into a farming family.

'They are wanting me to visit, but I don't know...'

It would be acres and acres and a lot of sheep; again, Roland would not fit.

'Margaret, my daughter, has been but doesn't care for the climate, too hot. I feel I would be the same.'

She mentioned her aunt, not to query the writing but because he seemed rather bereft, the son so far away, a daughter inclined to dominate.

'Mary was good to us when Helen was almost at the end: they were friends and she tolerated Mary when she hated other people seeing her as she was.' He sighed then smiled, as if he read her thoughts. 'I suppose later on we might have married, if she had wanted, but no.'

'It would have been a solution, for both of you.'

'Oddly, Margaret put her spoke in, took a dead set against Mary, of all people. But there was really no chance, she was faithful not just to the lad who was lost at sea, but to someone she did not talk about.'

That was something to think about later. She looked at photographs in a large album, all neatly captioned, wedding photographs, then Helen at Bridlington and later with a child, with children on the beach. Roland had taken those snaps but in others he appeared much the same, thin and neat and serious. She felt protective of him, rattling around in this house. 'You haven't thought of selling up and getting a nice flat somewhere by the sea perhaps, yet near enough for the family to visit?' A shake of the head.

'Not really. Of course Margaret and Tom would move in here like a shot but I don't want that.' Another smile, wry and humorous. 'I would be ready for Menston within a month!'

The asylum at Menston was another casualty of the times, but she knew what he meant.

Chapter 24

John was quick to see the possibility of Roland buying the house and handing over his own house to his daughter. 'Apart from being what she wants and keeping him independent, it might work well for tax purposes.'

He was a problem solver but he hadn't met Roland.

'The house would fetch a lot of money on the open market and he must be aware of that. If they were buying it, fixing a price would be difficult and just handing it over would hardly be fair on the son in Oz. And the stamp duty for this, the taxman wins whatever you do!'

'I wish I could have a word, persuade him and make my wife a wealthy woman.'

'If you met him you would see my point. The place is his life, the good as well as the awful part when she was ill. I can't picture him leaving, wanting the stramash...'

'Ah well! Madame has spoken, but it does seem obvious.'

'You have to feel sorry, the house is really big and crowded with furniture. He gets a cleaning lady in once a week but that can only scratch the surface.'

'There's probably an attic full of treasures...'

'And cobwebs, like Miss Haversham's. And he is a bit like her, marooned...'

Thinking of Roland and the lunch led to the question of food; were supplies lasting? Not as planned – carbohydrates and a lot of frying but not for long, then the brake could go on. They said good night. For once she did not want to open the olivewood box. She went upstairs and a little aimlessly checked things she intended

119

to take back with her. She collected one or two books and on a windowsill saw something she had liked, almost coveted as a child, and now of course it was hers. The horse, head bowed, the powerful arch of the neck, a foot lifted as if to paw the ground, a hint at luxurious trappings. The original bronze from some ancient Chinese dynasty would be in a museum somewhere or belong to someone incredibly wealthy but the replica was a brave attempt to recreate the beauty of it and a pleasant thing to have as a memento of the little house, of her aunt and herself.

In a cupboard were clothes left on her last visit and she took them out to rid them of the smell such a cupboard has when no one opens the door each day to take out something to wear. She would pack them, find boxes to fit in the car boot or perhaps large plastic bags. Downstairs there was very little, a few more books, nothing of value, furniture and kitchen stuff must wait, nicely arranged to give the right effect and charm the hordes of people desperate to buy... It amused her to exaggerate what the agent/manager had said, but only one person had to like the place, one with sufficient cash, and even that did not seem important, she was more concerned with getting back. Just tidying a house and waiting was a sort of limbo, a suspension from real life. On the farm she could be stretched to the limit, overwhelmed at times; her hands showed lack of care but in the north-east the Scots had a saying: 'A leal-he'rted lass wi'a guid pair o'hands is mair o'a bargain than siller an' lands.' When word came from Ilkley she would be off to prove it.

A brochure arrived by the morning post, describing the house as in a conservation area rather than in a 'conversation' one and the language was plainer, the layout better, it was well done. Loading the car, she heard the telephone and this time it was Margaret, Roland's daughter, wanting to visit. She was sorry to have missed the shared luncheon and wanted to put things right, keen to meet someone spoken of so warmly by Mary and now by her father. It was put forward with charm that she could come at any time to suit... The tray again and biscuits retrieved from the car and inevitably the thought that John was not alone in seeing the possibility of Roland moved to Burley and Margaret and family slotted neatly in where they wished to be.

The car was very new and Margaret's clothes were good. Of medium height she was not of the same build as Roland. Neither was she shy or diffident but soon at home, friendly and quick to admire the pleasant feel of the house, the unusual stove. She asked how one kept the rug so beautifully clean, she had never seen one like that with all the little bits, so colourful. Could it be vacuumed? Not easy to picture Margaret in the back garden holding one end of the rug, Roland the other and both shaking with vigour until they collapsed, laughing at the absurdity of it. Manicured hands and rings on plumpish fingers suggested Margaret's chores would be taken care of by a Firth figure carefully chosen and kept up to snuff. She too said Aunt Mary had been a good friend when the family needed one but did not mention any thought of a marriage or feelings about that which Roland had let slip. Civilised though the visit was, a not entirely pleasant feeling lingered, the impression of control, a quiet dominance like an iron hand in a velvet glove. The idea could be fanciful; however, if there was pressure on Roland she did not want any part of it. She went back to the task of loading the car and was closing the boot when Sandra came to the door and suggested a cup of tea.

'They're all out, thank God, I've the house to meself –

121

it might even run to a drop of something. You'll be off early you said?'

It was indeed to be early, not the crack of dawn exactly, but at first light with the idea of missing the worst of the traffic. Sandra had seen the visitor, guessed who it was.

'Boyfriend's daughter? Thought so! Does she want to move 'im in?' Another mind with a single thought.

'I don't know. It would be nice to sell to someone like him, knowing her for years, but he is hefted there, with all his memories, his life really...'

The moment of genuine sympathy for Roland's situation took a knock because Sandra didn't know 'hefted' and when it was explained she burst out laughing.

'You mean he's like an owd sheep? Well, you knaw best!' Sentiment was not uppermost with Sandra, life had not allowed that: divorce, children, a new partner, the past having to be left behind, good and bad alike. No memoir there.

But there was something she wanted to say to Sandra: 'Don't forget about the cottage, will you? You would be very welcome.'

'It is kind, but I dunno. Expect it'll be Benidorm as usual. Beach, bars 'n' bikinis – awful, but suits us and the kids.'

'You would brighten our lives in a bikini! Seriously though, the kids might love the farm and they could go to Crathie to see the Queen, Leanne would like that.'

'I'd like it – my mum brought us up to respect royalty.'

'Well, keep it in mind. We do get bonny days and there's always a guid dram to warm the other kind.'

They said goodbye as she would be off before their day began. Lying in bed, she remembered something that was not quite in keeping with respect for the royals. Long ago, she and John met a colonel who was very well-connected. He was particularly tall, probably about six inches more than six-feet and he had 'looked on the wine when it was red', becoming indiscreet. His tales of life at court had been hilarious, but the final pronouncement was a killer:

'Of course,' even the drawl was elegant, 'of course, you know, they are all DWARFS!'

Chapter 25

On the farm road it was best to watch out for sudden dips and loose stones everywhere. A friend from England said, 'My car suffered grievous bodily harm navigating your bloody road, John!' and got a cheerful answer that the aim was to keep rogues and vagabonds away. Apart from the cost of a splendid new road there was just a smidgin of truth in that. Anyway, she knew the bad bits and it was good to be home. She peered through the rain-swept windscreen to see if John had seen her and was waiting. He was not. She parked in front of a bull-pen and even there had no welcome. The old Angus was behind the wall of his querencia; rather than seeing him on his bed of high-piled straw, she could hear the gentle drone as he slept and maybe dreamed of his prowess on the braes when his turn came. John seemed to be elsewhere. The immediate need was a cup of tea. Into the quiet house to fill the kettle and lift the lid of the hot ring. Leaning against the warmth of the Aga to ease the ache in her bones, she rubbed at her neck, hearing it click as she tried to get rid of the stiffness. Taking longer breaks would have been sensible but she was home safely and that was the main thing; one or two of the roundabouts had bothered her, the Cougar particularly.

The tea was a reviver and she was pouring a second cup when John arrived. A welcome, and the hint of something more, good news, she could tell. The guess was right, there was a new calf, a fine heifer he said, one of the Angus cows in labour earlier than expected. High on the brae, he had seen the car and recognised the way she dodged the potholes, came as soon as the calf had sucked. Any addition to the strength rewarded all the care through long months of gestation. A safe delivery and normal suckling was savoured because sometimes it was not so – like potholes in a road, difficulties could arise.

John was merciful about the early morning feed, he would do it, would do it gladly being such a noble person and then after his slavery and her extra snores they could have breakfast, an enormous one, bacon, eggs, sausages, fried potatoes to make it perfect. Big eats to celebrate. Unless he was sickening for something, John's appetite never failed and perhaps it was catching – she felt hungry at the prospect. It was good to be back and hard to imagine his solitary breakfasts where speed and quantity would count rather than variety, the big eats mainly carbohydrate: the weaning process would have to be subtle.

John leaned back, loosening his belt by one notch, and emitted a gentle burp. 'Great, that!' he said. And it was, she had enjoyed both cooking and eating it. Spearing her last piece of bacon, she heard noise, from the road was it? John waved a piece of toast. 'What the heck?' He went to the gate and returned, shaking his head. 'You just can't credit it, can you? First flush of grass and here they bloody come!'

It was the ramblers of course, the first contingent. Scathing about supposed commitment to the Country Code after too many plastic bags, too many bottles and bits of foil, John did not look kindly on people walking on his property and left them in no doubt of it. A friendly encounter was unlikely.

'Finish your toast, I'll go!' Taking the bacon in her fingers, she went out, hoping to find agreement on the best route to wherever they were going. She would indicate paths in a civilised manner and hope for the same sort of response. It could happen. Beyond the steading where the road to the cottar house branched off, she waited for the people streaming towards her: haversacks, woolly hats, sticks with the handles carved as animals; grizzled old heads, middle-aged, and younger, though not the young and trendy who might choose more expensive exercise at the gyms in town. Harmless they looked, though as John said, they could be a bloody nuisance. All were putting a best foot forrard up the sloping road.

The leaders of the pack approached. By accident or design their headgear was plain, a deerstalker and a good flat cap dowdy in comparison with the followers. She wished them good morning and they stopped, remarking on the view, the Howe stretching away to distant hills, the dark shape of Bennachie easily recognised, and the river gliding under the bridge on the way to Aberdeen and the cold waters of the North Sea. Deerstalker was puffing a bit and seemed glad to listen while flat cap spoke.

'As you see we're a fine company!' waving an arm to include them all. 'We hope to reach Cairnheid the day!' adding that they were a works club from Aberdeen sensible of the 'fermers' needs.

She did not recognise the name of the destination, but saw a chance: 'And totally in favour of the Country Code, no doubt!'

'Of course, of course. We insist!'

They were willing to go the way she suggested along the path ahead and after two gates climb the brae to a further gate, then follow the high path to the start of forestry land. So that was all right then. Headgear touched in salute as they moved off followed by the supporting cast, some smiling and pleasant, admiring the day and

126

the view. On the right path, mindful of fences and gates, all good guys. She intended to point out how civilised the nature of the exchange, tact and goodwill all that was necessary.

She decided to wait for stragglers to give them the route in case the others got too far ahead. She called a cheerful good morning. A perfunctory nod came from the first man who frowned over the map in his hand and pointing at new and expensive fencing spoke forcibly. 'Yon fence shidnae be theeir!' He brandished the map. 'The richt o'way is clearly marked, beside the hoosie an' through the wee gate!' The tone bordered on aggression and made her want to kick pale shins visible below his kilt. She managed to speak calmly.

'Ah, I understand your point, but I wonder if you would be so good as to take the path along there and climb the brae later? Your friends did so willingly, it's hardly a step further...'

His face was red and truculent, thick brows of sandy hair came together over eyes that said not a chance. 'We'll jis tak the richt way, missus, accordin' te the map!' He headed off and the others followed, avoiding her eye as they passed, perspiring faces hinted at hours in the pub with too many drams chased by too much beer – no wonder they couldn't keep up! The thought was no comfort as boot after boot assailed the taut wire of the new fence. 'Vandals!' she wanted to shout as heads down they climbed, sticks prodding the slippery short turf on the brae.

Did they notice the mist of green as the larches followed other trees in leaf? Were they conscious of the stream bubbling a way down or old stone walls already starred with tiny flowers? Behind the dykes cattle were aware, long-lashed eyes missing nothing. Did they understand the curiosity of cows at any trespass? She walked back to the house, abandoning tact and goodwill for the time being.

Checking later in the day, John found the Blonde bull having a fun time in the company of yearling heifers, the window of opportunity coming from a gate left open. Apart from battery of the fence, all the stragglers had observed the Code, no detritus and every gate carefully shut: in no way could they be blamed for the necessary round-up of heifers to undergo pregnancy testing; the vet's bill was not their concern. The unshut gate was on the route taken by the first walkers and the culprit had to be in the deerstalker-flat cap gang. As an important lady Prime Minister said, 'It's a funny old world!'

Chapter 26

The bull frolicking with the yearling heifers had a fine-sounding name: officially he was Murdo Pride of somewhere impossible to pronounce except by the Scots. With no element of bad temper, Murdo refused to be removed from the pleasant company so unexpectedly offered him. Playful and yet determined, up and down the braes, along, around and about he led them, his feet had wings, he was Hermes, messenger of the Gods or he was Pegasus the winged horse, and with no golden bridle to hand they had no alternative but to take the whole lot, the hale jing-bang as the spik went, and put them in the steading where it would be easier to syphon Murdo off, bribe him with beetnuts, or somesuch. And they did just that. After which the heifers were returned to their park. Red-faced and exhausted, barely speaking to one another but with muttered invective about spring-heeled heifers and all morons rambling over the land wearing bobble hats, deerstalkers, flat caps or bandanas, they had gone back to the kitchen and taken a dram or two. Lifting her glass to the light, she reflected on the contrast between farm and village. Here a golden swirl in the glass after the hurled insults on the brae, there the easy talk over coffee cups in a quiet house. Sandra dropped a mild swearword now and again but the words from John had been unprintable, her own colourful enough: how could it be otherwise? For the child Mary, a naughtiness was 'midwife': words considered beyond the pale only a year or two ago are used freely on radio and television now, a trend to push back the boundaries, with heaven knows what result.

Deciding on an early lunch, she prodded the contents of the casserole from the oven. In twenty minutes or so it would be ready. With potatoes on the hob and broccoli waiting, she prepared the table and warned John: it was never too early for his big eats. The thought brought a smile and she began to forgive, Murdo at least. After a long, slow cooking the meat was tender and the gravy thick and flavoursome. John had a second helping and for once the potatoes remained on the table in front of him. The trials of his morning receded in a satisfying burp over a cleared plate. As an apology he murmured, 'Better a teem hoose than an ill tenant...'

There had to be an interval before the heifers could be tested but the time passed quickly in work-filled days never long enough to accomplish all that needed to be done. That was inevitable when the farm at one time would have had many workers in addition to the farmer and his family. Even modern machinery, contracted operations and casual labour never quite filled the gap. Sometimes there seemed a black hole into which time, energy and money poured with little reward. Then came days when things went well and every newborn calf was, in the words of MacNeice, 'a miracle after the ogre's night, And every sunbeam glad...' and blessings were counted. The sunlit bonny days had to be kept in mind.

When the day of testing came they hoped to manage without helpers; their vet, David, could be relied on to give the extra hand, and so it was. They brought the little band of playmates to the steading, fed a smidgin of hay to keep them occupied waiting for their nemesis and then syphoned off a few at a time into the pens in front of the building ready for the restraining crush. Volatile bundles of energy made fearful by the strangeness suffered the indignities and reacted violently, exploding into the holding pen after release: those more cowed found speed enough. Evident relief on all sides as John closed the gate on them back in their hill park. Return to the kitchen for a recap of the action, a look at bruises and a healing dram. David off to fresh fields. No casualties. Later John said, 'You know, with all the stramash, those bloody ramblers and all this I've scarcely had any news of the house and all the doings, as if the trip never happened.'

'It did, but the farm got in the way or at least the er, ramblers did. I'll have to think...'

She gave him more detail of the new arrangement and he was surprised there had been no pressure to accept the low offer.

'They usually want to strike while the iron's hot, clear their books, the loss is nothing to them.' John had a poor view of middle men. 'But what about Aunt M. – any goings on with the Otley chap? And his own fight, who's gonna win?'

She forced a smile because Roland was as innocent as he looked and what was troubling her had nothing to do with that gentle soul. She had been glad to be distracted by the hoo-ha, did not want to think or talk about it.

'There wasn't much else really. I read more bits from the reminiscences and have nearly finished. I think it's only two or three to go and of course the letters, I shan't read them ... I wouldn't want anyone to read mine.'

'Ho ho, what have you kept? Mine would be literary gems, well worth it.'

'So far as I remember all you ever wrote was "Sorry I can't get away", Buttercup or Polly or somebody was about to give birth!'

'But you caught me in the end! Happy days!'

He moved quickly, to dodge the answer to that, but she made no response.

Reminded that she would have to deal with its contents, with some reluctance she took the olivewood box from the windowsill. She sat for a time before choosing to open a book and once more enter into her aunt's world. In school holidays Mary had met up with her fellow White Ribboner and gone to Edna's house, finding Mrs Thatcher waiting at the gate in no mood for welcome.

Jus' look at the time! Where've you been? Ye knew you 'ave to take yer father's tea.' Edna didn't seem bothered.

'Can Mary cum wi'me? 'Elp me carry it?'

Edna's dad was an overlooker at the mill. We set off carrying the bag between us. Large bottles filled with tea and one extra with milk made it quite heavy. There were some packages in addition and one of them contained cake.

'Mi dad's gotten a terrible sweet tooth.' Edna seemed proud of that.

Along Main Street, down Iron Row and through the big gates to wait at the lodge because the lodgekeeper was busy.

Mr Fowler had so many waggons and lorries to deal with he didn't seem to know we were there and Edna got worried. ''E'll say "Tha's bin dawdlin' agean" an' we 'aven't. We'll jus' go!' She shouted over her shoulder, 'Mi father's tea, Mister Fowler, Weavin' Shed ...' Mr Fowler looked up over his spectacles and nodded. We ran down the hill, the bottles clanking together as the cobbles were so uneven and difficult for hurrying. I was impressed that Edna knew the way and did not go into the wrong place, Sorting, or Spinning, or any of the doors wide open at the time. But there was no mistaking the Weaving Shed, such noise! Women and girls watched the shuttles flashing from one side to the other through strands of wool stretched tight on the looms. People were rushing about. Carts rumbling along the aisles with spools of wool or finished bales. The lights were very bright and it was hot. Edna said the weavers were sometimes paid for a finished piece of cloth but if they made mistakes and the piece was spoiled they were paid nothing at all for their work. That was called Piece Work. They always shouted for the overlooker to help if they were worried and that was Mr Thatcher. There was no sign of him but one of the women called over, " E thowt tha'd gotten lost Edna!' Another said, " E'll be glad to see thee luv, 'is stomach's stickin' to 'is back!' I could hardly hear them over the banging and it was all so different from anything I knew then, strange and exciting.

When Mr Thatcher came, the first woman shouted, 'If ye skelp 'er ah'll git t'Bobby!' as a joke. Mr Thatcher said they were all full of blether and he took no notice.

Once out of there, the shuttles still banging from side to side in my head, I felt worried about the weavers making mistakes. I asked Edna if ever accidents happened and she said not very often, which was a relief.

That was about the last time I went anywhere with Edna because before we stopped at her gate she said, 'Since goin' te t'Grammer ye don't talk like us. I thowt ye looked down yer nose a bit in t' Mill.' I felt very hurt because I certainly hadn't, I was dizzy with the noise and heat and it made me quiet, which I suppose was unusual. After that misunderstanding it was never the same.

Chapter 27

It was an effort to continue when all she wanted to do was to forget, leave the past out of reckoning, take the box and dump it out of sight, but that would take some explaining and any way it would be stupid, STUPID in Mary's terms. She could not shirk but might skip a lot, the pleasure had gone...

The book covered early years at the grammar school, at first giving facts, the amount of homework expected, how easy or hard Mary found it. Then one or two new friends appeared with nothing of hindsight about the descriptions, suggesting they were taken from diaries kept at the time, as had occurred earlier. Catherine from a middle-class home, admired for her 'golden hair flicked back as she talks and her face goes pink if you tease her'. Likeable Kathleen, 'a bustling sort of girl exactly the same age as me. She tries to keep up with our group in gym but her legs are short and she cannot balance very well but she is very jolly.' Mary helped a girl called Irene struggling to keep up, found ways of slipping her the answer to sums or spellings, but the most important new friend was Harriet. Fascination with Harriet shone from the first mention – 'She is quite tall and rather thin, her hair is brown and fine and curls at the ends and her eyes are strange, not really brown and sometimes quite golden, but very big in a small face.' Later, Harriet's influence became clear.

We got detention from Miss Horsfall for talking in Scripture. Harriet says it is all bosh and we should not have to endure all the twaddle and I was only telling her to shut up and stop muttering when I was caught, but Harriet owned up as she is very honourable. Anyway, we had to write out a hundred lines and of course miss the school bus and so we walked through the park, calling at the tuck shop. I like to choose from the penny or ha'penny tray but to my surprise Harriet said, 'Don't waste money on that stuff, if we pool it we can get some cigs.' And we did. They cost twopence-ha'penny for five. She already had matches and we smoked as we walked. It felt very exciting but I dreaded anyone seeing us and reporting us to the Head. I kept coughing and Harriet guessed it was my first time. She says she has smoked for ages and prefers it to eating sweets. Her smoking started when she went to the riding school next door to help muck out one Saturday.

Aunt Mary only occasionally smoked a cigarette, so a habit was not formed on that momentous day. Religious belief was something less easy to verify, but she did go regularly to the parish church as the years went by and new names followed the Palmer-Patersons of her childhood.

The diary excerpts tailed off until the classes became mixed for the brighter pupils and boys were in the reckoning. Catherine of the golden hair acquired a boyfriend and blushed more than ever, Kathleen was popular with the newcomers, Harriet not so, did not like it when Mary was admired and was waspish about the admirer called by a nickname, the real name not given. One day after school he walked with Mary through the park where flowers were in full bloom and swans drifted on smooth water above the weir. The footpath on the old bridge was so narrow they walked singly and then the street was busy and they separated and again in the passage reeking of beer leading to the main road. Both carried satchels heavy with homework. They exchanged a few words about the flowers and the swans and nothing more. At the bus stop they smiled and said goodbye. Innocence shone from the page. Choosing to copy this excerpt, perhaps Aunt Mary was conscious of something lost in later sophistication.

With examinations looming, anxiety took hold. Her mother, seeking to limit the time spent on study, came to realise that failing to cover the work set had a more adverse effect than putting in the effort to complete it and Mary worked into the small hours.

Entries about the teaching staff were brief but telling – an early one about the headmaster:

Mr Robins is very grand. He sweeps down the corridors his gown billowing out like an avenging angel. His face is pale and he has long sideboards of hair. He does not smile.

Mr Padgett is really nice. He is not handsome or tall, in fact his face is ordinary and he wears thick round glasses but he is so good at making you understand difficult things I prefer him to anyone else. At first with the lady French teacher I did well enough but now I really love the classes because of the way he brings everyone into the lessons; he knows everything that happens in school and out and brings that into the conversation in French. He teases Catherine about blushing and once when I tripped in the corridor he told everyone that a damsel fell at his feet one day because she had been drinking beer out of a bucket. I never forgot that in French one drinks 'dans' rather than out of.

I get infuriated in maths because Mr Cummins conducts all the lesson at the speed of John Smith, the brightest pupil. I cannot keep up and guess it is the same for some of the others.

Mr Watts likes Harriet. I think it is because she is very blunt when she answers him and he finds it amusing. He has very black hair and a brown face and really beautiful white teeth and cannot help smiling. All the girls like him and try

136

to get his attention. We think it is a pity he is married and keeps getting children. He would make quite a good film star though he is not really tall enough. One day a girl called Doreen knew the answer to a question he asked and it was the name of a town in Kenya, Kisumu, but when Doreen said it seemed like Kiss me and everybody burst out laughing. She may have done it on purpose.

History lessons are becoming a joke. We do all the studying at home because the lessons are so boring. He hardly seems to recognise that we have exams looming up, in fact we learn hardly anything and are in danger of failing what should be an engrossing subject. We grumble but put up with him which is easier than making a complaint. They say he is going to retire soon. I wonder what he was like at first.

Opinion was no less frank about female members who were not up to snuff: the teacher of botany came under fire:

Miss Buxton is very pretty and always seems flustered as if she is not too sure which class we are and just where we are in the curriculum. Sometimes we start to cover the same ground as in the previous lesson and she apologises very prettily but it all wastes time. Harriet says she has a lurid private life and spends all her free time in nightclubs, which I am sure is imagination run riot. Harriet spends a lot of time at the riding school talking to girls who are much older and tell her peculiar things.

There was an earlier look at Miss Buxton during Mary's first term, when she sent Mary on an errand to the chemistry laboratory.

'Mary dear, will you go to Mr Nield and ask him if I can borrow a water bar?'

137

Now what was a water bar? Unused to a southern accent Mary had tried to repeat the exact sound of the strange requirement. There was no help from Mr Nield.

'...Water bar? Water bar? What on earth is that child?'

Total confusion until the penny dropped.

'Oh, you mean a water beth!'

A young woman and an older man were employed to educate the young. They spoke with different tongues because the places where they grew up were widely distant. Their baRRth and bEth were foreign to the bAth of West Riding folk. It was a pity that vulnerable Mary should be a go-between.

Chapter 28

The exams came and went and for Mary that was almost the end of school life. In the last week lessons were perfunctory, teachers and children knowing the die was cast and no more to be said. During one of these relaxed classes Mary gave rein to mischief unsuspected except perhaps by Harriet, who knew her best.

In our last lesson with Miss Forster we were half-heartedly discussing poetry and she got us to read poems, one verse each round the class. It was a bit boring and no one made much of an effort. I worked out which verse I had to read and decided to mis-read it to liven things up when my turn came. It should have been 'wrinkled with age and drenched with dew, Old Nod the shepherd goes' but I said Old Sod the Neppard, making a Spoonerism of it. Miss Forster looked aghast at first, I suppose because it was me, but then she burst out laughing.

During another lesson the headmaster summoned each pupil to his office. This appeared to be the only time the headmaster interviewed a pupil, other than after some misdemeanor or other. Apparently parents made the choice as to whether you stayed on at school or left to take a job. No careers officer, no discussion of further education or financial help to that end. For school-leavers responsibility had ended, a job depended on what was available and what you could find for yourself. Bright children must have slipped through the net when parents could not fund them, and Mary was one such. Her interview with the headmaster was a travesty:

I felt shaky outside the door and he did not hear my knock so had to call a second time for me to go in and was annoyed. He asked if I was leaving and when I said, 'Yes, sir' that was that. There is no chance for me to go on with things as they are, I need to earn money but could not mention that. He said, 'You should look for an office job' and I said, 'Thank you sir' and left. The most unlikely people are staying on, some not expected to do well like poor Fred, popular and beautiful to look at but thick as a plank. A bit comic really.

In the headmaster's study the relaxed joker had reverted to the earlier self, unable to communicate with the awesome man behind the desk. In fact there was a brave acceptance of her situation and nowhere does she seem to bemoan fate. It is hard not to judge the headmaster, though perhaps he was just a man of his time.

As it happened, a job came easily to hand when a young woman living nearby who worked at a printing machine firm in Otley was given a promotion and suggested Mary as her replacement. After an interview Mary, finishing school on Friday, started life as an office clerk the following Monday. Fait accompli, at a promised wage of fifteen shillings a week.

That particular information was familiar, used at length by her own parents to shame her into getting down to school work. 'You don't know your luck,' her mother had scolded when teachers complained about lack of effort. 'Think of your poor auntie, distinctions in almost every subject, but having to leave and...'

...'go to work for fifteen shillings a week,' she had dared to mock to make her father laugh, knowing he would take her side.

140

Writing still provided an outlet for Mary. Though the Scottish dictionary defines 'chiel' as fellow or older person, she was the 'chiel amang ye takkin' notes' of Rabbie Burns. The first working weeks produced thumbnail sketches of new people.

The managing director bustles about. He is sturdy and thickset with a very red face and short grey hair. He works hard and everyone jumps to it when he is about...

Another older man has almost the same build but very pale. I do not know what his position is yet or which is his office. He looks stern. His name is an old-fashioned one from the Bible. He is obviously important...

The man who interviewed me is the secretary. He seems nice, on good terms with everybody in the main office, though I am not in there. He said I should do very well working for Mr Alfred in his office, but other people might ask me to do things. I hope I can manage everything. Mr Alfred is on holiday just now...

Three other directors share an office at the front of the building. One of them is nice-looking and said good morning when I passed him in the corridor. I haven't seen the other two yet.

Later all came under closer scrutiny:

One of the typists was fuming in the staff room about Mr E. She said his name was from the Bible but he was a miserable old bugger with no consideration for others. She had to work late doing a whole document again because she made a tiny mistake in the first version. She wanted to leave early to meet someone she is keen on who can be awkward at times. I hope I never have to do anything for the Bible man...

Two of the directors in the front office do not come in every day and usually arrive later than the M.D. or Mr E. I understand they go abroad for the firm sometimes but neither gives much work for the main office. The other one is more often in the works...

I have spent the first few days in Mr Alfred's office just tidying it up and checking some catalogues. Once I was asked downstairs to learn how to use the telephone switchboard. When Martha suggested I answer one of the calls I was not at all keen but managed it. I would not like that job. On Friday I have to go and help with the wages...

At last Mr Alfred is back. He is tall, thin, with fair hair receding a bit, and a pale face. When I found out he was the son of Mr E, I dreaded him being the same but he is quite shy and speaks softly and asks would I mind doing whatever it is, rather than telling me. I like him. There is a second son in the other works all day but sometimes he comes into our office. He is dark haired, also going back at the forehead, in fact dark complexioned altogether; he is serious looking but not cross. Both are concerned with the works and wear white coats which get pretty grubby by the end of the week.

One of my jobs is to handle the wage sheets from the shop floor, recording the details weekly. It is simple to do, the only snag being that some cards are covered in grease marks. The foremen from each section bring them to the office and it is interesting that some have taken trouble to keep the cards clean whereas others haven't bothered. You can tell by the foreman's appearance what his cards will be like...

I had not thought of the exam results being in the paper and it was a surprise when there was a knock at the front door which we don't use much. Mr and Mrs Palmer-Paterson saw my name and came to congratulate me. I was confused and bent down to pat the little dogs when they asked, 'And what next Mary?' They looked confused to hear me answer that I was already working. They asked kindly after Mother and would have come in but I said she was asleep, hoping it was true...

I found the day in the wages office interesting. It was busy, with a lot of people from the works coming and going but all very easy and no hassle. The boss there is tall and thin and is a relation of one of the directors but everyone calls him by his first name with no mister attached. Not me, of course. His assistant is a young man I have seen chatting to the typists who tease him about girlfriends. Martha the telephonist likes him. He is affable but shows no particular interest in anyone...

I am getting to know people from the main office. We meet at break-times in a room set aside for female staff. A woman comes in to make tea and coffee and she is a great source of information about everyone in the place, especially the big noises. Some of her gossip is unrepeatable and I am resolved to take it with a pinch of salt. Harriet would love her. I met Harriet's mother in the market place one lunchtime. Friendly as ever, she hoped I was enjoying my job. I believe she really disapproves but hasn't the faintest idea of my situation. Harriet has stayed on.

Chapter 29

The routines of office life lost novelty and became familiar. In a move to the secretary's office, grubby cards and kind Mr Alfred were left behind, not without the tinge of apprehension usual with Mary, but all went well. More in contact with the directors, their qualities and foibles did not escape scrutiny, tetchy Mr E included.

I had to get some figures out for Mr E and he seemed pleased, which was a great relief. He is usually very pale but I know he gets angry and goes red in the face if you get things wrong.

Accuracy, clear handwriting and neat entries in the various books were noticed and more tasks were handed over to free the secretary for other things. He confided to the senior typist that his new girl was 'an acquisition', which was duly passed on and pleased Mary's mother. So there was success in the job but the home situation was deteriorating:

I need to find someone to come in while I am at work, just to check. I can pay but will it be enough?

The writing more fragmented, the odd line about a typist leaving to get married, but little except the Christian name of her successor, Lily, and then blank pages...

The inevitable had happened. For so long it was the two of them, Mother and Mary; the brother sent to Canada on what was intended to be a prolonged holiday had fitted perfectly into farm life, as good as adopted by the relations there. He was sent back briefly but Mary, truly bereaved, was most affected. A tiny pension gone and little in reserve, when everything was paid nothing remained. Mary's increased wages could not fund the rent, leaving no alternative to giving up the house and going to live under Aunt Lizzie's roof. There was no little book about the new situation. From Aunt Mary herself and from family gossip half listened to as a child she had some picture of that time. In contrast to growing respect and promotion in the office, there was no home life in the true sense. Many moons later Mary joked that she paid the accepted rate for board and lodging in shillings and the rest of the obligation in tears and sweat. As often in humorous talk, an underlying bitterness was clear. Small wonder she did not put into words what it was like being there as a poor relation. From her own meetings with the cousins as crotchety and petulant old men, she could not imagine them deliberately cruel to Mary; selfish and thoughtless from lack of a good example might be nearer the mark. Aunt Lizzie being something of an auld besom, for her it would be normal to want the maximum return for the sheltering roof: in effect, she acquired a servant for herself and her family.

Dennis reappearing on the scene must have seemed heaven sent, a literal *deus ex machina* on a BSA 350cc motorcycle. Childhood friendship resumed and at last someone on Mary's side to give a sympathetic ear. It was easy to picture the two of them on the quieter tree-lined roads before motor traffic took over. No crash helmets then, so did his hair glow ginger under a biker's leather cap with flaps for the ears? Was the face pink and freckled still? And Mary, was her hair short, in a bob? And what covered it, a scarf tied under the chin, so unsafe in today's terms? How difficult was clinging onto his back on the twists and bends of the Dales roads? Did they walk, attempt Pen-y-Ghent or Whernside? Or, swift as the flash of grey walls and greening slopes offered to the speeding bike, did time defeat them? A girl more confident, able to put her foot down, refuse some of Aunt Lizzie's demands and stop being at the boys' beck and call? She fancied not. Somehow or another all would be fitted in by getting up earlier or working later, the hours with Dennis sweeter without guilt. A career in the Navy was to separate them but offered a future with prospects and anyway the threat of war was on the horizon. Dennis would serve in any case and preferred to do things his way, the life at sea more attractive than anything else on offer. So a parting came and eventually so did the war, but nothing was recorded.

Looking again, she realised she had read the books in the wrong order but it did not matter, Aunt Mary had copied from diaries, re-read the pages of neat handwriting and at times added comments or further notes. A record made but with the sequence not too clear, a bit of a jumble like life itself if you think about it, no perfect order even for someone like her. Fiddling with the books, she realised that on the faded covers were numbers so faint it was no wonder she had not seen them. Somehow her pleasure in the writings had vanished and now she was going to have to face that fact and why it was so.

John's face came round the door: he was apologetic. 'Would you mind breaking off to look at Flora? I am not easy about her and someone's coming up the road, it looks like the laddie from the college.'

She was glad to go, to be in the fresh air and take the high path to find the herd. The braes were greening and after a lot of rain growth would quicken. Heavy clouds threatened still but moisture on the dykes sparkled in gleams of sun; a cold breeze brought the smell of pines from the planting on forestry land. The herd was in the far park, scattered in search of a bite. They needed sun as everything did, crops, pasture, all creatures great and small... And there to offer balm to the soul, the Howe, widespread to distant hills in a chequerboard of farms, cottages, trees, stane dykes ... but on the fringes of memory was something infinitely troubling that would not be soothed by any fine sight.

She found Flora grazing, seeming normal, but it would be as well to make sure, look at every animal but come back to her, keeping an eye on her all the time. That was part and parcel of the job, constant surveillance, making sure, looking at possibilities. Maybe farmers would make pretty effective spies, a perfect sideline to earn more money. What a thought, become a member of MI5 or 6, or why not the KGB or whatever name it had at present? The qualities required – stamina, persistence, an eye for possibilities – nae problem at all. A cow lifted her nose and raindrops fell from thick hair on her neck; friendly, biddable Beauty, particular favourite. 'Fit like, lassie?' It was John's way of greeting all the coos and she had adopted it. No trouble with Beauty nor any of the others. She went back to Flora and thankfully it was the same after careful checks of udder, feet, gait. Long-lashed eyes blinked under the attention but there was nothing to report. She went back by the river parks, having a look at the Angus cows on the way. All in order, but the river was high, swollen with all the rain, debris bobbing about in it, bits from trees to be fished out at the arches of the bridge as a farmer's perk, logs free to hand rather than bought in. A small blessing to add to the rest.

Chapter 30

She woke early with feelings she didn't care to identify. The clock face read four o'clock. She looked at John sleeping the sleep of a farmer who needed more help than he could afford and more rest than he ever got. So wide awake that sleep would be impossible, she decided to get up.

The stair creaked ... all sounds magnified, a thunderclap of water to fill the kettle, clatter from the Aga lid. Welcome warmth in the kitchen and the tea scalding her mouth. Nothing to be seen outside.

From the olivewood box on the windowsill she took books and letters then returned the books in the correct sequence though it did not matter. Two piles of letters stared up at her, those with foreign stamps and the few later ones with strange markings and coded numbers from the war would be from Dennis. What she told John held good, she did not want to read what passed between the lad and the waiting girl. Without disturbing faded ribbon keeping them together, she put them back: the beautifully crafted hinges allowed the lid to close with no sound at all. She refilled the cup and waited for the tea to cool. An envelope marked 'His letters to me' remained on the table. Found in a bedside drawer with other things – glasses, aspirin, sweets, Scholl's cream – obviously the writer of these letters was not Dennis, his were safely in the box. As if spoken yesterday, Roland's words were endlessly in her mind, had led to this pathetic huddle over the stove at an ungodly hour, with a cup of tea now too cold to drink... 'She was faithful not just to the lad lost at sea, but to someone she did not talk about...'

Wrapped from prying eyes, but there when sleep would not come. 'His letters to me' – who the heck was this! Queen Elizabeth mourning Dudley, sweet Robin? Also married to someone else? Spiteful to think like that but she could not help it... Head in hands, she sat until a break came in the darkness and blackbirds rustled the garden hedge. Then, making an effort, she refilled the kettle and took down the frying pan. Bacon sandwiches would be best, the smell drifting up the stairs to alert John before the alarm went off. They could eat before going over to the steading, put themselves first for once.

He came dressed ready to start work but more than willing for bacon nicely crisped between a slice of toast and one of thinly buttered bread, her compromise for the thick wadges fried when she was not there. He gave a close look at her but blessedly made no comment: it was one of his many virtues that he was not a morning talker, coos most in mind then. Other things were usually left until coffee time. She put the plate in front of him.

All in all the day went smoothly, with no effect from the scant hours of sleep. She took on most of the steading work while John went to mend a dodgy fence which had been a worry for some time. One small panic when he came back to get ropes and her help with Dolly, who had fallen into a ditch. The search for a fresh bite over a bank made sodden by the rains had resulted in a reach too far and collapse under her weight. It could have been disaster, a broken leg or worse, a miscarriage, but after rescue she stood, rolled a mild eye at them and eventually began to graze.

'I'll be about an hour clearing up, shall we eat early?'

'Why not? We started early enough! It's a casserole, ready more or less, except for the tatties.'

That was the way of the big eats, nothing learned from

149

the chefs on television, only the simplest of dishes prepared in advance to be heated up – soups, casseroles, vegetables done at the last minute and easy puddings, fruit or cheese. Not a diet for slimming but what a trauchled fermer relished and needed, plates always cleared. She had cookbooks, Raymond Oliver, Pellaprat, John Tovey from Miller Howe in the Lake District, ubiquitous Jamie, but elaborate stuff would have to wait, and wait.

After eating the evening meal a last check on all creatures, geese to be shut away from Reynard aware of the little family and only too willing to stop their chunterings. Then with luck, time to watch television, have some music or perhaps just talk ... but tonight she did not want to explain anything, convinced the matter was hers to sort out. King Alfred's dictum again, she firmly believed in that. John would take over as he was apt to do, the 'dominant partner' someone described him, and she had laughed, knowing it to be true.

As if in answer to thought, the noise of a Land Rover pulling up outside the steading sent John to see who was there and he came back with Jim Raeburn, a neighbour from a few miles away.

'You'll take a dram?' Hardly a question, more a statement. She proffered cheese and biscuits still there from the meal and they settled at the big table, talking as always of the weather and how the beasts were doing and the markets, leading naturally to what folks thought of the 'bluidy government'. In Jim's opinion the present lady Minister was 'nae wirth a docken, the rest twa-faced lawyers jist.' No challenge to that. Glasses refilled with the golden liquid known to be the water of life in the Howe and other fair places on earth. With preliminaries over, the reason for the visit emerged with a slip of paper taken from a jacket pocket. Straightening it out, Jim explained.

'My lad Davy is hirin' himsel oot, that is on his vaycation, ye ken. Sax hale weeks o' et he'll git an' sair anxious he is tae earn a wee bittie in that time. He's a gran wirker John an' if ye shid need a han' onnytime theeir it is ... an' the pey he'd require aa written doon as weel.'

John took the paper. 'I'll be in touch, Jim. Can always do with another pair of hands, being married to a lazy woman...'

Blue eyes twinkled at her, 'Nae missus, that's nae richt, a'body kens that.'

She slept reasonably well, not surprising considering the long, long day and the distraction of the visitor. Her mind was almost settled about the letters but work came first and later there would be time. John had noticed.

'Feeling better after a good zizz? Nothing like it.'

Walking to the steading, he promised to make use of Davy. It was a nice thought to start the day. After routine jobs she decided to muck out one of the pens and John went to finish the fence in the far park, another item to clear from lists they made. One of these days household jobs will figure, go to top place she warned, but both knew it was an illusion.

At the end of the day, while John fiddled with the television trying to correct its many frailties, she took the packet from the drawer and slid half a dozen letters onto the table, registering without surprise her father's handwriting on the envelopes. As a tiny girl he was the one taking her to Number Six just for an hour or so in what had seemed a happy arrangement when her mother was so busy with one thing or another and glad of the respite. There had been jokes and a lot of laughter and sometimes her father talked quietly with Aunt Mary. One day she had been allowed out to play with children from the house opposite but had fallen out with them and

151

come back in tears to tell them, but they were upstairs and came down a bit flustered and she had seen her aunt's pretty hair was loose round her shoulders and her father was cross and said she shouldn't be such a cry baby and try and get on with other children. Going home he had been bad-tempered still and told her not to worry her mother with chattering too much. There had been other times like that before they moved away but she had forgotten, let them drift out of mind until Roland and then a photograph of Mary showing a fine head of hair.

John looked up as she lifted a lid of the Aga and then exposed the glow of the fire. He made no comment as one by one the offending letters dropped and melted away in the fierce heat. In a voice that sounded a little odd even to herself she said, half-laughing... 'Now is the time for the burning of the leaves.'

'Show me where that comes from... '

She went to the shelf where she had left the books brought from the village house, most of them paperbacks, including cheap anthologies of poetry, very early ones, the pages loose, binding coming adrift.

'It's Lawrence Binyon, in one of the old Penguins. I'll never find it ... but it is apt. I read a lot on my "holiday" and that one I liked particularly ... "time for the burning of days ended and done... Let them go to the fire with never a look behind" ... Just what I'm trying to do.'

'Well, the funny thing is...' He was searching in his pockets and came up with a crumpled newspaper cutting. 'This was in the local paper on Friday and I meant to leave it on the desk. Thought you'd like it.'

Quoted to illustrate an article, without naming the source, the poem was in the Doric:

'Div ye nae mind?' they speer an' I say Na
I dinna wint tae mind on aa that's by.

I've mair tae dee nor fash wi' fit's awa.
There's naebody can cheenge it, onywye.
I dinna wint tee ken fit's gyan tae be.
I'll seen ken aa aboot it fin it's here.
I hive the day, an' that's eneuch for me.
Yestreen? The morn? Na na, ye needna speer.

She smoothed the creases in the cutting. Later she would copy it into the Commonplace Book.

Chapter 31

Farm work took them over when calving began, time-consuming and exhausting and rewarding as always, with the familiar problems arising. Good strong calves were born and were nourished and protected by good strong cows, but now and again a poor weak calf did not survive and gave some heartbreak or a rogue mother would not suckle. They worked their way through until only one or two cows were without progeny and life became easier. Operations for the re-seeding of a park were completed and a contractor employed for the planting. The farm cycle relentless in its demands, weather of vital importance in everything, particularly for the new stock. A lot going on with the farmhouse at the centre, the telephone insistent as arrangements were made, cancelled, adjusted. Casual workers were called in and paid promptly. Contractors sometimes could not hold to a promise made and tolerance was stretched to the limit. Tempers flared but in most cases good relations were preserved. Frustration made worse by tiredness; times when muscles threatened to seize up and the spirit wavered. The life they had...

Not to be forgotten, the farm books. A plethora of facts to assemble and post off to the Min. of Ag. Rules to observe, note and register in the mind's compass. VAT, forms, tax forms, forms concerning membership of the European Community. Sometimes the little house came to mind, the silence and the peace there as it waited to have meaning again, someone making a home, painting the faded walls, refurbishing and bringing it to life. Cherishing it.

She was coming to terms with what she had been so reluctant to face about her father's importance to her aunt, acknowledging the fact without dwelling on it. Being overworked had the advantage of leaving her too tired to think. Like John, she slept without interruption. In a Walt Whitman poem one of the many merits of animals is that they do not 'lie awake in the dark and weep for their sins'. She was too exhausted to weep for her mother.

When every cow in the herd had a calf, twin calves or an adopted calf there was time to catch up with things neglected during this key time on the farm. Above all they could have and enjoy a more normal pattern of work. On one of these more relaxed days Postie brought a letter from the estate agent telling of renewed interest in the house after the local press carried the fresh advertisements (copies enclosed). A not-so-welcome enclosure was the bill for the amount the advertising had cost. Before she had time to write a cheque, Postie delivered more news: her friend had the pleasure to inform her that offers had been received (copies enclosed), and he awaited instructions. To her surprise, the offers exceeded the price fixed originally. There was a choice of immediate acceptance or waiting to see if better offers were made. The decision was her own but she wanted John's opinion. When they settled after 'aa was deen' they could discuss it.

They arrived at a solution. She would answer the letter saying she intended to come down to clear the contents of the cottage and would talk to him then about the offers: this would mean delay of only a few days while arrangements were made. The great thing about it was

155

that John would try to get Jim's lad Davy, the 'gran wirker', to look after the farm and he would come with her. This time the holiday would be for them both, a very rare happening, and all depended on Davy. With the boss away from the farm, a lot of information was to be left about routines to be adhered to if possible, together with details of cows and dates of calving, any treatments given, name of vet, useful telephone numbers, and so on. A suitcase packed, vehicle at the ready, just the word from Davy required. When it came Davy and his father spent time with John going round the farm. They asked questions enough to satisfy him he was leaving the coos in good hands. Dad coming along was a bonus: there would be an informed second opinion if the young man needed it.

So, bright and early one fine morning, a holiday began. Good progress to the Forth Bridge and a steady run to Lauder where a fine pastry shop offered nice things to supplement packed sandwiches and they took a break. St Boswells. Jedburgh and on course for Corbridge. The rather monotonous miles of that stretch led to talk of the legacy.

'I think I was a bit miffed she probably didn't leave it to me for myself, more for him...'

'No. Not really, mostly for you judging by the will.'

'That bit about me was added later, but it doesn't matter.'

Mile after mile of straight road, too narrow for the traffic, smallish fields, low hedges... She returned to the subject. 'Were you surprised, my father being so rotten?'

He frowned and shifted a little uneasily. 'That's not fair. It's a helluva long time since, but when we first met you tolerated him as Jack the Lad, but now you can't stand knowing it got too close to home...'

The diesel engine thumped into consciousness the truth of it and the lameness of her excuse: 'What about my mother? I hate it for her sake more than mine.'

He seemed to be concentrating on the driving.

Coming home after college she had made fun of her father's ladies, blind to her mother's anger and frustration, didn't see it or had refused to see it. Now for the first time in her life she put her mother first and was ashamed...

The road was busier and John really concerned with traffic. After a while he spoke of food, he would be skeletal before they got anything. She looked at the maps.

'Skeletal is not a word for you... When we get to the A1 it will about twenty-odd miles to Ripon, we could get something there.'

Really she couldn't care less but it would be best to stop, have a change of scene: she was spoiling the trip for John and being a drain. She resolved to snap out of it, be a radiator instead ... just like Daddy-O!

Chapter 32

A high tea, which in Scotland would have been called a fish supper, followed by a stroll and then a long look at the cathedral made for a late arrival, and without noise or lights the terrace seemed asleep. One small house had disturbed the run of John's days, made them harder by removing his 'slave labour' and of late preoccupied that slave not altogether happily. Putting down the suitcase, he stood in front of the old-fashioned range, the vase beside it waiting for tall flowers; all the things he knew about made real – rug, sofa, bookcase emptied of treasures – and he felt out of place, the room too small and himself too big. He waited while she took a sheet of notepaper from the mantelpiece, unfolded it and then looked up, smiling.

'It's from Sandra, saying "Welcome Home" and that she popped in to put the electric blanket on. Isn't that nice?'

Sleep came easily after the journey and all diversions along the way, and a morning was before them with nothing except a telephone call to be decided on. She knew how odd it would feel for John, so rarely away from the coos.

'When I've seen the agent we can decide what to do. Go anywhere, walk perhaps?'

She was determined not to spoil things for him, but in truth as soon as the door was unlocked the walls of Number 6 had breathed betrayal, her aunt, her father, the whole sorry mess. She needed to go out.

A surprise from the agent, who said another offer was likely if she could wait, he would know quite soon. She came out of the office and found John looking in shop windows unlikely to interest him. Coffee at Betty's added to the unreality; they were tourists, on holiday like others at the immaculate rather crowded tables, deciding in a desultory fashion what to do next.

Walks by the river. Skipton on a market day, farmland on the journey there, sheep the mainstay, very few cows. Otley for another market day and then Leeds by bus; the arcades, more recent shopping centres and unique as always, the market. Supper with Sandra and family and an answer to the question asked previously: would they like to have anything from the house? It had to be cleared, the new people, whoever they were, would want a clean sweep. Sandra liked the old-fashioned brass bed in the spare room and the sofa to replace their old battered one but wanted to buy them, which could not be allowed: in return for all her kindness they were a very small thank-you.

The new offer on the house did not materialise and she accepted not the higher offer but one made by the young couple she imagined going for a smart new apartment furnished with white sofas and a tall vase with a sunflower. Perhaps they had to lower their sights, but at least would have a roof and a 'feature' range. She decided to leave them the rug and the vase to take sunflowers.

John had refrained from telephoning Davy too often but she could tell the charm of a holiday was fading fast. Sherry was not the drink for a Scotsman and clearly 'Ye'll tak a dram?' not the norm in Ilkley, so he was not impressed as she was to see the agent open the drinks cupboard on the closing of the deal. There was just one more thing in mind before they went back home and it would be good for them both.

After a fitful night culminating in an unpleasant dream, she woke when the light came through curtains not fully drawn across the window. There was something of a completion in the fact that never again would that shaft of light awaken her and whoever slept in this room would be in a different bed with different sheets and covers; the room itself could lose its pale colours and contain other things. The shade of Aunt Mary would not be at home here.

The dream that helped to waken her was a garbled reconstruction of a visit to Number 6 when they came north to attend Grandmother's funeral. The three of them had left the house where relatives were gathering and at her request had walked the short distance to see Aunt Mary, whose front gate had not opened easily and there had been a pause before they walked up the path. In the dream her mother became violently agitated and lunged at her father who stood white faced except for vivid spots of crimson on his cheeks. 'There, you see?' a finger pointing, the voice harsh, unsteady with hate, ... 'The flush of shame, my girl! Remember it!' The horrible part of the dream was that she clearly remembered odd colour on her father's face as he fumbled with the gate. Nothing else, her mother's firm profile impassive during a civilised visit. How could you explain dreams, the nastiness containing some tiny shred of truth to make you trawl back through memory, wondering... Quite awake, she decided not to get up when all too soon they would return to the early starts and all the mouths waiting to be fed. She snuggled down into the warm bed and returned to thoughts of her mother's handsome face giving little away except

160

displeasure when opinions clashed. Other emotion seldom registered, but what pain was hidden? Her mother so busy with community affairs that she never felt close, and she herself, relying on her father's regard, had made no effort.

And the husband and father, his ladies and the attention he got from them, was he also estranged by ever increasing committees, a plethora of good works, the church? Wherever they moved it was the same – home life secondary, the household well organised to fit in with all the rest, yet somehow cold. She remembered in Aunt Mary's writing the uncle shifted outside because his smoking marred a spotless hearth. Was it like mother like daughter, her father and herself similar nuisances in the way not of household gods but of good works? For the first time in many months she tried to think of him in the old way, full of life and hardly ever serious, with all the blarney, basking in the attention he attracted. He kept interest alive by being different, a little outrageous, making people laugh. Quite elderly ladies blushing, 'How can you say that?' Smiling through downcast lashes, a girl pouting, 'You are so rude to me!' It had seemed funny at the time, she could remember giggling at the impact he made and telling her closest friend, rather proud of Jack the Lad. But to be fair there was more to him than that sort of flummery and men found him good company. So far as she knew he never made an effort to help in any of the good works, yet he was the one to light up a room with the huge smile, the bonhomie. The wanderings from the straight and narrow were they what the French would call *passades* and not too serious or had some gone further, as with Aunt Mary? Perhaps the oddest thing was the marriage itself, how did it come about with the two of them so different? She seldom thought of her mother being in the same mould as Grandmother, yet in different circumstances and more subtly the controlling factor made her a prime mover, likely to set her sights on him rather than the usual way round, the biter bit as it were: she was smiling at the ludicrous idea when John woke up.

'Ah, pleasant dream was it?'

'Hardly, I was just...'

'...thinking you were walking in a fine garden and there, striding towards you, was a man in a wet shirt?'

'Could be!' She might have told a fib, not wanting to confess she still raked over the old bones, knowing full well it was time to stop. 'Aa the folks is deid onnywye!' would be the message in the Howe.

Her plan for the day was to walk on the moors; she wanted to remind herself how lovely it was and re-discover the uniqueness. All who walked there found it special, but after so many years was it the same? She reckoned it was unlikely the heavy hand of 'progress' had reached so far. After a good breakfast they would set off; the day looked promising.

Chapter 33

The house clearance was pretty thorough and left very little to be loaded in the car for the return journey. Taking the planned route, John drove faster and always more confidently than she did. Responsibility for the farm and animals was a powerful incentive to get home but in her case there was relief at something coming to an end, a chapter closed by the sale of the house. For a long time the engine hammered ... ended and done ... ended and done ... and with every beat the weight was lifting from her shoulders. She wanted to reassure John her silence meant she was just thinking and not brooding, and made a start: 'The little man who cleared the house was nice I thought and pretty quick about it.'

'And the sons. A shock about the teeth... Did you notice?'

'O Lord, I guessed you had. Two with only a half a set. I tried to see the young one but he never spoke...'

'Probably the same. A discount for a job lot. Useful!'

It was easy to expand on that and it brought more elaborate and sillier ideas until traffic increased enough to require concentration with Newcastle ahead. Past there they took a break in a place said to be 'up-market', to them an alien concept as applied to a collection of houses and shops. There was no evidence from scrawled graffiti and unhinged doors in the public lavatories; litter shifted about the car park as if the breeze itself lacked resolve. Everything suggested the better part must be elsewhere.

Chance to relax, an occasional solitary figure crossing to reach another parked car the only distraction. Sandwiches and coffee from the flask and time to ask, 'What did you think of Number Six? Was it a good buy for them? It did seem smaller with two of us...'

'Well, as long as they don't overeat!'

'Hmm ... gannets should talk!'

She brought up the question she really wanted answered: 'Did you get any vibes there? I don't know how much you remember about my aunt? Things went so adrift for me when I found the letters I couldn't see straight, it all seemed so rotten...'

He was silent while an elderly couple passed, faintly smiling as people do who are comfortable with their day and not harassed by the clock, then answered, 'She visited so rarely. Seemed to approve. Of me as well, which your ma never did.'

'We didn't let that interfere!' Oblivious of other people, she had known John was right for her and determined to learn how to cope on the farm.

'A good job the visits were infrequent.' Recalling how they softened reality by sprucing up the house and themselves beforehand and tried to keep her away from any hassle, he grinned.

'We cleared sharn almost before the coos dropped it. I used to wonder if I carried the whiff, showered more often just in case!'

Her father had been unconcerned, except at the distance between them – Scotland was the back of beyond to him. She returned to what she wanted to know.

'With both my parents, you saw between them...'

'Dysfunction. They were ... different.'

He was loth to say straight out they were chalk and cheese, her father the charmer with all that implied, her mother quite the reverse, a closed book even to her. It was best to leave it at that. The village was safer ground. 'What about the "gateway to the Dales"?'

Hesitation and then half-laughing, 'Not for me! Couldn't stand it! Houses on top of one another. Kids everywhere, bikes, skateboards ... I was dreading you wanting to hold on for holidays, the ones farmers don't take. You know that.'

With the closest neighbours a distance away from the high farm, animals, wild things and acres and acres of space all around, time at college for him and for some of his friends their only absence, the sole experience of crowded living. She had started off in a village but lost count of moves in the south to cities, people, shops, all the amenities and the drawbacks. Like her parents, their meeting up was unusual but between them, thankfully, a world of difference.

'Time to get under way.' Overfull waste bins in the car park explained the drifting litter and confirmed life could have existed at an earlier time of day, but soon the question was left behind, the car eating up the miles again on the featureless part of the journey – small fields, hedges, nothing to interest or excite comment.

'I forgot you could hop off at any moment, with all your "brass". Is that the word?'

'Yes, you'll have to watch out.' Up to now it had been pointless to think about the money. 'How would you spend it? Besides on coos?'

'Can't think, maybe a bull to replace the auld Angus.'

'Consider it done.'

Other ideas came to mind and were discarded until, 'Increasing our kedge anchor would be good and then perhaps something permanent like planting trees ... if you agree we could find a space?'

'Good notion. Very good indeed. You should have a bit of frivol too, clothes and stuff.'

'I dunno, perhaps shoes...'

They fell silent, lulled by the monotony of a long journey lacking interest because mile after mile change becomes meaningless. Her mind wandered back to the village and the perfect last day, calm and clear with just a hint of cold to make it right for walking. Striding along as if going to find the herd, John in his element at last. She made an effort.

'I'm glad we got the moor walk in.'

'So am I. It was great!' The recollection amused.

'I can see why you fitted into the farm so well – a mountain goat on the tops! Made me feel tired!'

'That was a compliment then?'

More miles, another stop for a rest. Little talk. The offer to take a turn at driving refused: 'No fear, I want to get home before midnight.'

For once she could not bother to rail at the way men, John particularly, regarded women behind the wheel; it was nice to snuggle down, try to take a nap. She reflected on the sale; it was odd to think of the young couple she had discounted from the start being the eventual buyers. Were they in the house now, getting the feel of it, putting a match to the fire and as the flames grew and warmth spread savouring their first home? Though of course if the sofa had gone, Sandra might be the one relishing the comfort of the Arthur Darb... For a while she slept. Awakened by a difference in movement as they approached a roundabout, it was good to see a train crossing over the Forth Bridge: a short spell on the motorway and then they were truly on home ground.

Still occupied by thoughts of the house, she hoped her aunt would not have minded the sale but knowing the farm was her life, it was unlikely she would expect otherwise. Turning to her father's importance in her aunt's life was less easy but had to be faced. Really she knew nothing at all except how serious and lasting it had proved. The memories raked over were less than pleasant and she wanted rid of them. Perhaps time would bring more perspective: there were good things to remember and it was a pity to lose them. One thing to decide on was the memoir, what to do about the writing so faithfully and for so long recorded. Again, it was something for later.

'Come back, have you?' John brought her into the present. 'What are we going to eat when we get home?'

Chapter 34

'There's No Place Like Home' – a ballad with a message which drifted from drawing rooms to smoke-filled bars and then across the world, having power beyond genteel sighs or an exile's tear or any tipsy blub. Thoughts of home eased the last miles of the journey, with every bend in the road familiar, the map tucked away. They spoke of Davy waiting or more likely gone home to be in touch later; wondered what was the quickest and easiest thing to eat and whether to look at the cows before or after they ate whatever it was. Fetching farm supplies from Aberdeen or after shopping in Inverurie, the choice usually favoured the cows and, aware of that, often she changed from shoes to welly boots in the Land Rover, quite a manoeuvre.

'He did say all's well, when you phoned.'

'Yip. He said "Nae problem", to be exact.'

'Such a relief, I can't wait...'

He did not remark on that but seemed amused for some reason.

At last the village, with houses along each side of its lang stracht, not in a cluster like the Yorkshire one. Soon the tricky turn onto the lane leading to the bridge and the routine dodge of pitfalls on the farm road. They were home. It was natural to move to the bull pens before opening the garden gate: the old Angus cudding peacefully and raising a mild eye to them did not trouble to get up.

'Certainly nae problem there!'

'He hasn't noticed...'

Perhaps it did not matter who filled his manger and refreshed his straw or groomed him occasionally, as long as these things were done to keep him well content until his turn came on the braes.

The coffee pot blipped and wafted its promise round the kitchen, ready for Davy to report on his days in charge. He had enjoyed it, appreciated the spread of the land, the quality of the cows, particularly the pedigree Angus herd building up. They discussed the difficulties of the old steading and what John had done to try to adapt to the present day. One thing only had bothered Davy during his tenure, and that concerned people.

'I had a visit. The stots were fudderin' aboot an' I found kids in the steadin'! I was fairly mad at hoo the hell they got there an'I nivver saw. Nae deein' damage, jis' wanderin' roon haein' a keek but it was the scraichin', fu' blast...'

'On their own, were they?'

'Na. I was jist giein' them a tellin' when the mither came with her dander up an' she made a richt steer, set all on 'em jumpin'. An' me! God what a woman!'

'No dad then?'

'Och ay. He cam haudin' oot there's nae trespass in Scotland an' they could go weerivver they liked! Bluidy cheek! They stay at Drumkindie, bocht the manse hoose theeir. They're English!'

'They would be!'

A look from John swivelled in her direction. Davy, too intent on what happened next, had forgotten her origins.

'Onnywye I stood my grun. Told the kids to git out an' waited till they were awa'.' He breathed hard then began again. 'Bit ye'll nivver guess... Wha's theeir wi'a picnic? Twa days efter? Only the hale faimly, like lairds jis, tablecloth an aa, by the river! I wis flamin'...' He still flamed a bit. It was John and the hikers all over again. 'Sae fit te dae ... I got on the blower to Dad. That's his auld muck-spreader ye've seen ahin' the steadin'...'

It was plain to see the pleasure of spreading muck with the wind in the right direction to put lairds o' the manse, wives and children and picnic baskets to retreat, vanquished by means of an honest smell.

'Dad said ye'd ken we thocht it the onny wye, folks like yon ... I'll tak' the machine noo. I doot they'll be back.'

'I'm more than grateful, Davy, for your help, most of all for that.' John rummaged in the cupboard and came out with a bottle of malt. 'Give this to your dad and thank him for the loan. Best idea ever!'

She broached the subject after Davy left. 'I guess you'll be looking out for something of the sort?'

'Maybe so. I got rid of ours when I got Wullie to the muck, hadn't thought of that use for it.'

'A shame when people can't have a nice picnic...'

'My heart bleeds. By the bye, I know that particular dame. Face to stop a clock and the voice to shatter glass. I heard her yelling "Damon! Dancer! Dizzy!" at dogs who didn't give a toot, totally out of control and a bluidy nuisance to everyone, including the witch herself.'

'I take it you are not fond of the English?'

'Only the well-heeled ones.'

It was a pleasure to check the herd on such a day, John taking on the climb to the high brae, her lot easier, going to see the Angus cows. Davy had moved them to a fresh park and they were grazing purposefully, the sheen of

170

good health on them. She knew at one time the Angus had been the mainstay of the farm and that John, mindful of tradition, tried to keep a reminder of it while having to follow the market and use a continental bull on bigger cows. She walked around, stroked or rubbed at the tailhead if allowed, talking, using the name as John did. With all in order she took the high path; it was a day for meandering. John was not in sight, so she sat down in a favourite place where larches made shade. The Howe stretched out. An early mist lingered on a pattern of fields, stone buildings and dykes and clustering trees repeated until it faded beyond sight. As if all took breath there was little movement; grazing animals were painted on the green squares, toy tractors made no way on road or park. The bonny days had come and the Howe offered its best guise. John arrived: all was well on the high brae.

'Stay here a bit, there's no hurry.'

Perhaps days away from the farm affirmed that living and working in such a place was luck beyond measure and this day demanded awareness of it, hinted that work could wait. Below them the river was peaceful, all urgency forgotten.

'You said your river was moved!'

'The scars healed, but a lot was lost...'

'Not necessary here...'

'Thankfully.'

She had been reminded and wanted to make certain she was forgiven. 'I've been a bit of a pest, I know!'

'Nae problem!'

'I shut you out, got the hump – the house had an effect...'

'Natural enough.'

'At first I felt guilty she left me everything and I didn't deserve it – the place reeked of loneliness and I'd done so little... Then later of course I got mad, thought I was just a substitute, giving it to me as his flesh and blood, not for myself at all!'

'I guessed that.'

'And you hit the nail on the head. I was jealous, of both in a funny sort of way. What an idiot! However...'

'Let's go and put the coffee on and I'll tell you what the whole thing reminds me of.'

The kitchen needed tidying but it wasn't the day for it. She filled the pot and measured out the spoonfuls, noticing she would have to grind more beans for the next break. John had spread himself in his battered old chair, his feet over the corner of the table.

'Go on, then, I'm waiting...'

After a moment he spoke, fixing her with a direct look. Gently he began: 'Once upon a time there was a schoolgirl,' a brief smile, 'quite a skinny lassie, I gather, with pigtails and a pale face.' He took the mug of coffee, sipped and put it down smartly because it was too hot. 'This lassie had her ear bent by a pal whose doctor told her to exercise a shoulder that was really broken!...'

'I think I see...'

'Don't interrupt this fascinating insight. This wee lassie could hardly walk home because her own shoulder felt so bad...'

'Don't go on. I've got the message!'

He was aware she had taken unto herself the solitary life of her aunt, as good as widowed by the war, vulnerable to the close, the familiar charm. She could see now the way it was, but the damage had lasted a lifetime because no one came into orbit to cancel it out.

She went to the Aga to get refills of coffee.

'And all of it in the past. Both beyond caring, Mum as well. Stupid to get upset he wasn't quite the hero I made him!'

172

He was smiling. 'In one sense your father was unlucky, not having the right wife like me!'

'Mm. That's true, and Mum didn't have the luck either, no farm, no coos...'

'I could tell you were longing to get back. It seems to me you're properly hefted!'